Sundancer's Joy

Sundancer's Legacy - Book Two

Elsie Davis

Psalm 119:28
My soul is weary with sorrow; strengthen me according to your word.

Chapter One

♥

A lmost home. Or at least the nearest thing Erica wanted to call home.

She nodded to herself, feeling relieved. Erica reached for her cell phone and called her aunt. "Good afternoon, Aunt Mary. Just wanted to let you know I'm about twenty minutes away from the house."

"Oh, good. So, Gabe found you okay at the airport?" her aunt asked.

"Yes. The big sign with my name on it was easy to spot, given how small the airport is."

"He's the son of Nancy and Fred Myers. You remember them, don't you? Anyway, he was kind enough to offer to pick you up."

"I think I remember them. You can't imagine how much I'm looking forward to being back in

Juneau and with you and Uncle John. Quiet and low key…just what the doctor ordered, and exactly what I want for myself."

"I'm so excited you're going to be staying with us for a while. Quiet and low key are definitely on the menu…at least…soon enough."

Erica frowned. "What do you mean by soon enough? Promise me you don't have anyone at the house. I'm so tired." Not to mention, her leg and foot were throbbing with intense pain as she hadn't taken more pain medication since boarding her first flight from Raleigh, North Carolina, earlier this morning.

"Oh, dear. Please don't be upset with me, but there are a few people who want to see you. I'm sorry." Her aunt's voice held a deep note of worry…and regret.

Erica pushed her disappointment aside, needing to show gratitude to her aunt and uncle, not selfishness. At sixteen, her parents filed for divorce and moved back to the mainland. It hadn't taken long to get fed up with the bickering and fighting. Even now, it was stressful talking to either of them on the phone, so lost in their own worlds they didn't have the time of day for their only daughter.

Luckily, her parent's non-involvement allowed her to spend summers and school holidays with her aunt and uncle. Those were the best times, even with Erica's own case of a broken heart keeping a chokehold over her happiness. The *not knowing* what went wrong managed to keep her praying for an opportunity to run into Adam. *Her sort-of ex-boyfriend*. Of course, she never ran into him, seeing as his folks ran a wilderness guide business based in some remote location near Taku-wok, a small town about a half hour northeast of Juneau.

"It's fine. Just promise me that when the conversation starts to lag, you'll help encourage the people to leave." Erica chuckled. Entertaining was the last thing on her agenda, but it wouldn't be the first time in the last few months she had to suffer through the pain in silence. The only thing worse than the pain was the pity she often received from others when they realized the extent of her injuries. It was also the reason she tried not to use her cane, much to her doctor's consternation.

"I promise. Whenever you've had enough, we'll leave. See you soon, honey." Aunt Mary hung up the phone before her aunt's parting words sank in.

Leave. Why would they leave the house after the impromptu social hour?

Erica shook her head, knowing she'd find out soon enough. Gabe had little to say, but it gave her the opportunity to relax as he drove toward town. She spotted the green *Welcome to Juneau* sign, and her spirits rose a notch. Juneau held a lot of wonderful memories, but unfortunately, the counterparts for *wonderful* were downright miserable. Which is why she enlisted in the Army at eighteen right out of high school. Her focus had been to be the best that she could be. The Army's motto stuck with her at every twist and turn of her career. *Until now.* Her best might never be good enough again, but it's not like she had a choice. A healing broken leg, and multiple fractures in her foot and ankle that suffered permanent damage, would forever limit what she could and couldn't do.

Used to being active and deployed to military hot zones, a desk job stateside wasn't her idea of a lifetime career, which is why she chose not to reenlist. With her military career over, there was nowhere else she wanted to be other than here. Ever since her return to the United States, this was the moment she'd been waiting for. *A chance to start a new life...fresh, with no mistakes in it.*

She was right back where she started...in Alaska. Only this time, jobless, damaged, and nowhere else to go. At least she didn't have to move in with her mother or father in Washington. Tolerating either of them for more than a day was out of the question, as it continued to be a one-sided relationship that Erica refused to subject herself to with any frequency.

And no more doctors or surgeries. Two painful surgeries to repair her left ankle and foot and a hard cast on her leg to stabilize the fractured femur, she hoped to never step inside a hospital again. Or limp inside, as the case may be. The injuries had left Erica with a permanent limp and a cane to get her through the bad days.

Generally speaking, Juneau would be quiet in the off season. Unfortunately, tourists would begin arriving in another month, and she would have to weather the influx of people until late summer. Erica prayed she would find peace during her visit, something that for months now had evaded her completely. Nights were the worst, but she hoped being away from all things military, the nightmares would end.

After ten years in the Army, Erica was back to being a civilian. No more rucksack runs. No more trenches. No more early morning drills. No more of all the things she had grown used to over the years. Do *your best* was the motto she had lived by, always planning to make the military a lifetime commitment. And what did she have to show for the ten years now that it was over?

Nothing worth anything by her way of figuring.

Commander Wilkens had awarded her the Purple Heart for her actions the day of the explosion, but the cold metal did nothing to make her warm or make her feel proud. There was nothing that could help Erica understand the death and destruction that came from her last days in Afghanistan, and the part she played in the moments before it happened.

The GPS announced a left turn ahead, and Erica snapped out of memory lane. She scanned the area, but instead of houses and scattered piles of melting snow on the lawns, she saw businesses. Hank's Gas 'n Go. Tilly's Grub and Brew.

The Alaskan Trader. *Wait…what?* This wasn't the right direction for her aunt and uncle's home. Erica leaned forward to get Gabe's attention. "I'm sorry, but it seems you've made a wrong turn. I'm going to 562 Bear Cub Run, which is back the other way on the outskirts of town."

"No mistake, Ma'am." He smiled into the rear-view mirror. "This is where Mary Turner asked me to bring you." The young man pointed out the front window and slowed down.

Erica leaned down lower to see better out the front window.

Welcome hometown hero, Erica Carter. Big red letters were splashed across the banner that was hung across the street and attached to the tops of two lamp posts.

Erica swallowed hard. Throngs of people had gathered and were milling about in the general area. She was tempted to tell the driver to turn around so she could make an escape. This was the worst thing possible. The need for quiet and low key was certainly on hold, as there would be no quick exit. Her aunt and uncle meant well, but this was over the top. She wasn't even remotely close to a hero and hated the very word used in connection with her name. If she had been a genuine hero, two soldiers wouldn't have died in the explosion. That they were good friends of hers made it even harder to stomach.

God, please grant me the ability to do what's right and the fortitude to get through this party I don't deserve. All she wanted was to fade into the background, hoping to heal physically and emotionally. *One more hurdle.*

She pushed her hair off her face and behind her ears, hoping to quell the rising panic. Her throat felt full, like a balloon was lodged there. Erica silently counted to three, but it didn't help. Nausea threatened to unload the small lunch she had eaten at the last layover in Seattle. She closed her eyes, trying to fight back against the anxiety. *One more hurdle.*

Erica pictured her favorite spot...Mendenhall Glacier. She imagined the seagulls flying around, seals floating on the icebergs, and the majestic beauty of the iceberg calving as large chunks of ice broke away, falling into the chilly waters where it would float for days or weeks, going who knows where. A place she photographed so many times, she had lost count. Her love of photography was another joy that had been ripped away from her life by the explosion. It would seem there was nothing left of who she once was. It would be like starting over with a clean slate. Erica wished she could turn back the hands of time, but knew it was impossible.

Heaving a heavy sigh, she scanned the faces of the crowd of people waiting for her to get out of the car, their smiles and laughter like salt on a wound.

"Ma'am, are you okay?" Gabe's voice brought her back to reality.

"Yes," she lied. Her aunt and uncle had pushed through the crowd and were nearing the vehicle. Time to put on her game face. She massaged her leg and foot, hoping she wouldn't embarrass herself getting out of the car. With one last disdaining look at the cane laying in the seat next to her, she grimaced and ignored it. When she used the cane, the curious and sympathetic stares doubled.

Erica zipped up her parka and slid on the fur hat she'd picked up during her Anchorage layover. She opened the door and slid out, putting most of her weight on the right leg and using the door frame for support.

"You're here. Welcome back to Juneau, sweetheart." Aunt Mary enveloped her in a warm hug, her breath a cloud of vapor in the cold April temperatures.

This was something Erica had looked forward to, and it helped inch her bravery upward to face the others waiting to see her. "Thank you. I can't believe you did this." *Wished they hadn't done it, not that she would tell them.* Erica turned to hug her uncle.

"We are proud of you and once a few people found out you were coming back, it kind of spiraled out of control. Everyone wants to celebrate you and all that you did while you served our country."

Except they were glossing over the fact she didn't save all the soldiers that day. "Thank you, Uncle John. It's very kind of everyone. I'm just a little tired from all the traveling. It'll be fine, I'm sure."

They headed toward the crowd, and several rounds of cheers erupted. Erica cringed, forcing a smile to her face as she waved. The pain in her foot was excruciating, but she wouldn't let it show.

Soldiers didn't complain.

Or so she'd been told.

"Hello, Mrs. Watson. It's so good to see you again." Matty Watson had been one of her favorite teachers during her junior year in high school. Even with only three schools and small classes, teachers came at a premium as not everyone wanted to live year round in Alaska. And when Erica stumbled over algebra, Matty jumped right in and tutored her after school until she figured out the disconnect.

"Welcome home, dear. We've missed you." At least Matty didn't mention the obvious injury or bring up the incident. Erica preferred not to discuss what happened...with anyone. Especially not after being grilled by the commander, doctors, and the psychologist. Everyone wanted the details of the incident, and she'd been forced to relive and repeat the story so many times. It was then, the nightmares started.

And hadn't stopped.

After Matty moved off, the same process continued over and over until Erica couldn't bear the pain in her leg and foot anymore. She hobbled over to the drink table, grateful for the sure-footed soles of her fur-lined boots. Grabbing a cup of hot cocoa, she then sat in the first chair. Not many folks had left yet by the looks of things, but if anyone else wanted to talk with her, they would need to seek her out…while she remained seated.

Aunt Mary and Uncle John checked in on her occasionally, especially her aunt. The worried look on her face made Erica try harder to make the event a happy one. Movement to her left caught her eye, and she checked to see who had pulled up a seat to chat. The sun was behind the man, and she had to squint to focus, trying to figure out who he might be.

"Hey there, stranger. Welcome back," the man said, his voice husky and yet familiar.

Erica froze. Ten years later, and she still recognized Adam Landon's voice. The same voice she recalled many times over the years in the dark dirt trenches. She and her comrades would spend long hours in them as they took turns protecting makeshift base camps from the enemy.

"Thanks," she said, her voice crisp and cold in direct contrast to his friendly one. What she hadn't counted on in her recollections was that the senior with zero facial hair from high school would become devastatingly handsome with what could only be considered scruff. Almost like a five-o'clock shadow...from five days ago. The mustache didn't hurt either. *Not that she cared one way or the other.*

It was one thing to play a role for the friends of her aunt and uncle and the folks in town, quite another to keep the false persona for Adam. *Her first and last love.*

One stolen kiss at summer camp, then the guy vanished from her life as though there had been nothing between them. Except Erica knew better. She'd fallen in love with the eighteen- year-old camp counselor, and if he was to be believed, he loved her too. It was only after camp ended, Erica realized Adam had lied.

Cold disappointment left her wondering over the years about his defection, despite that he was the one she pictured to help make the loneliness not so lonely throughout her military career. A face in the darkness to bring light. At least he had been until she found out he was engaged while reading through the Juneau local e-newspaper on her phone.

Adam raised one eyebrow in question, a quirk she remembered from high school. But why would he expect any other greeting? And for that matter, why would he even dare show up here? A man who should be married and probably had children by now.

"What's it been, like eight or nine years? You look good, kiddo. Other than the lines of tension deeply embedded in your forehead, that is. Coming back to Juneau will be good for you," Adam said, half a grin on his patronizing face.

"Perhaps, Dr. Landon, and it's been ten...but who's counting?" Erica added dryly.

"Wilderness guide, not a doctor," he countered.

Erica frowned. "I thought you had big plans to go to medical school?" She couldn't help but ask, not that she was interested in anything about his life.

"I went to school in Anchorage for a couple of years. But then life changed directions when my parents died and left me the business." The smile on his face disappeared.

"I'm sorry. I didn't know." Adam would have had a hard time with their deaths, as he was close to his parents. Unlike the relationship she had with her own mom and dad.

"There's a lot you don't know, having been away so long."

Erica frowned, his enigmatic comment confusing. As a detail-oriented person, she liked to keep in the know, which was another reason the surprise welcome-home party had thrown her for a loop. She had never liked surprises...even before the explosion.

"I'm sure my aunt and uncle will catch me up to date over the next few days." Erica was at a loss for something else to say. Too much time had passed, and they weren't kids anymore. "So do you live here, in Juneau?"

"Yes. A few years ago, I bought a ranch house on the outskirts of town. It's bigger than I like, but a necessity. At the moment, anyway."

"I wouldn't have ever thought you would move to the city. And what about your business?" Small talk about jobs and the weather was always a safe topic.

Adam shrugged. "People change. And Juneau's not exactly a thriving metropolis. I still have the wilderness guide business in Takuwok, but I've got a friend who runs it for me now. Gilly's good with people and loves living remotely, so the arrangement worked perfectly. I spend most of my time in Juneau working on a project."

More elusive comments, but Erica refused to show interest. "I see." She didn't, but at sixteen, eighteen-year-old Adam hung the moon. Not so much anymore, married or otherwise.

"You look tired. Are you sure you're feeling okay? If you need to get out of here, I would be happy to drive you back to your aunt and uncle's place. My truck is right over there," he said, pointing to a huge blue Chevy parked on the street.

Adam's truck was more like the monster trucks she saw on TV. Sort of. The wheels were bigger than normal, but not humongous. It still looked like a toy truck to her. "That won't be necessary. And by the way, that's the nicest compliment I've heard all day." *Not.* She frowned, rolling her eyes at him.

"I'm not trying to insult you. Just noticing that you seem like you would rather be anywhere other than here." He used to know what she was thinking, and the fact he still had the same ability was a bit unsettling.

Erica nodded. "I am tired. Jet lag has a way of doing that."

"Then let's get out of here. I'll let them know. There's no sense in you sticking around for hours while the party winds down and then to sit through all the cleanup while you wait for a ride."

It was a nice offer. An offer she was tempted to take, even though it was from Adam. Erica peered at the crowd, then nodded. "Won't your wife be upset if you leave without her?" He hadn't mentioned his wife, not once, which was disconcerting.

Adam frowned and shook his head. "That won't be a problem, seeing as I'm not married," he said, his voice flat. It was as though he'd retreated to a dark place.

It would seem the marriage was short-lived. "Well, okay then. I would appreciate a ride to my aunt and uncles. Any chance you can get my things from the car I arrived in?" She didn't enjoy asking for help, but she also knew her limits. And it would be easier to make her way to Adam's truck without his intense scrutiny.

"Sure thing."

"It's the black car over there," she pointed.

"No worried. The truck is unlocked. Meet you there."

Adam was gone in an instant, preventing Erica from changing her mind. She hobbled toward the truck, trying to ignore the shooting pain in her foot and leg. If only she'd used her cane. Pride had a way of mocking her at the worst of times.

Standing by the truck, Erica realized there was one enormous problem. *Getting in the truck.* She would handle the challenge the same way she did every other challenge in life...with grace and dignity, if possible.

Several minutes later, she gave up. *So much for grace and dignity.* Adam was taking longer to return, and Erica was tempted to bolt.

Chapter Two

♥

Adam unloaded the two suitcases from the trunk of the car and then scanned the interior, not wanting to miss anything important. He spotted a cane leaning against the back seat, wedged under the front. He grabbed the cane, unable to imagine why Erica wasn't using it. The lines of pain around her eyes were visible to anyone who cared to notice. Pride sometimes pushed a person too far, and in this case, he was certain Erica fit the bill.

Originally, he hadn't planned to go to the welcome-home party, knowing seeing Erica again would be awkward. Except not going would have drawn more attention, and he wanted to avoid having to make explanations...or excuses. One of the drawbacks of remote small-town living. Of course, there was a tinge of curiosity.

After meeting sixteen-year-old Erica at the Nanooka summer camp, he had fallen for the energetic, meet-life-heads-on camper who showed up for riding lessons demanding he teach her everything. No simpering young girl, her zest for experiencing life far outweighed even his own. As a camp counselor, however, anything other than a friendship was off limits...at least until after camp. Just shy of eighteen and graduating, the world had suddenly looked brighter with Erica in it. Adam had fallen hard and fast for the young brunette with short hair that framed her adorable face.

Except any plans they had of getting together after camp were squashed by Erica's father instantly. Two years apart in age wasn't much when you got older, but apparently, while still in high school, it was a huge deal. Unwilling to even give them a chance, Adam had given in to her father's demands out of respect. Soon after, he had been shocked to discover that her parents had moved back to the mainland and gotten a divorce.

Eventually, Adam's feelings had faded, and in college, he met Natalie. Falling in love with her made him realize his feelings for Erica would most likely come under the category of a crush.

Adam started for the truck, surprised to see Erica still standing next to it, her arms bundled around her as she warded off the cold afternoon chill. The passenger door was wide open, but that's as far as she'd gotten. Erica checked to see if anyone was watching, then moved forward, grabbed the interior handle and tried to pull herself up. A feat made impossible because it would require her to put her injured left leg in first and bear the weight as she pulled herself up and in. Adam hurried to her side, recognizing her dilemma.

Erica looked up at his approach.

"Sorry it took me so long."

She bit her lower lip, something she did when she was uncomfortable. "It's fine. I didn't realize how high off the ground your truck is."

"It helps me get around in the wilderness, off the beaten path. But I see the problem." He pushed her two suitcases toward the back of the bed and then moved around to the passenger side. Holding out her cane, he was surprised when she didn't immediately take it from him.

"Toss it in the back with the suitcases. I don't really need it," she said, though her tone was unconvincing.

He did as she suggested, but then scooped her up in his arms, taking her by surprise.

"What do you think you are doing? Put me down, right this minute," she huffed.

"Relax. It's either this, or you can stay at the party for a few more hours. There's no way you can climb up in the cab with your injured foot."

"I'm sure I could have figured it out," she insisted.

Prickly little thing. "Maybe, but this is easier. Buckle up," he added for good measure before closing the door. The comment earned him another irritated frown.

Adam slid into the driver's seat and started the truck.

"Everything okay with my aunt and uncle? Were they upset I was leaving?" Erica asked, concerned about how they would take her sudden departure.

"They were fine, and completely understood. Talking with them is what took me a little longer, as they were worried about you. I kept reassuring them you were simply tired."

"Okay...and thank you."

"You're welcome."

The stark silence in the truck was unnerving as he wondered what she was thinking. "Talkative, aren't you?" he asked, coming to a stop for a red light.

Erica shot him a look that could freeze hot water. "We have nothing to talk about. So why pretend? You have some sense of guilt perhaps that brought you here today, and maybe you think giving me a ride is your form of apology for the past. I just want to get to the farm for some downtime, even if it's on the back of a wagon hauling pigs."

"Remind me not to force you to talk." Adam chuckled, though the barbed insult struck a raw chord he wouldn't let her know. "We were friends. More than friends, if my memory serves me correctly. Granted, we were kids, but still. Once upon a time..."

"Don't say it." Erica shook her head and exhaled deeply.

"What? I apologize for the way things ended. I wish we had talked before you moved out of town. Circumstances prevented me from seeking you out, and then everything else happened so quickly."

Erica crossed her arms, her lips pursed, and her nostrils flared. "You've got a lot of nerve. You kissed me," she hissed. "You made me believe you cared and then ditched me like a bucket of dishwater. Turns out, it was the best thing you could have ever done for me, even if I didn't like your methods at the time."

He had never seen this side of Erica. She had become a beautiful woman, but clearly full of emotions and feelings that had seen the darker side of life. She didn't pull any punches, though admittedly, he deserved her anger.

Sort of. "I had my reasons." None of which she knew.

"I'm sure. But don't worry, because like I said, you did me a favor. I wasn't the fall-in-love type and didn't want to get trapped in small-town living. Instead, I got to see the world via the military. I loved my life...until this happened," she added, pointing to her foot, her voice breaking on the last word.

It would seem he had been the only one with a broken heart. "Good to know. So, we've settled the past between us. Surely, we can be friends."

Erica let out a heavy, steady breath. Was dealing with him so bad, or was it something else? Lines of tension etched her face, and they bothered Adam. Once upon a time, Erica's vitality was enough to make anyone feel alive being around her. Now, not so much. It was as though life had been sucked out of Erica.

It struck a chord in him that continued to resonate and wouldn't let go. He wanted to understand what had happened in Afghanistan. Wanted to make things better. Chalk it up to the protective side of his nature, something Natalie appreciated about him. However, he was almost positive Erica wouldn't appreciate his help, given her response to him even assisting her into the truck.

"What's going on with the leg and foot?" Adam asked, figuring it best to get the elephant out of the truck. It was the only way he could understand and figure out how best to help Erica recover from the emotional wounds she was hiding.

"None of your business. You and everyone else know all you need to know. I was injured in an explosion. People died. I got an honorable discharge and now I'm back in Alaska. End of story."

"Not quite how I heard the tale. You're considered a hero and earned a Purple Heart for your bravery. So, what's the rest of the story?" he pressed.

"Some soldiers were saved. Others weren't so fortunate. The loss sucks the joy out of everything else. Happy? Now you know. End of discussion," she said as they pulled up to the house.

"No, I'm not happy. You're clearly hurting, and whether or not you believe me, I really cared about you once and find I still do. As a friend. So don't pull the brushoff with me and expect to get away with it."

"Cared about me? I don't think so. Maybe during camp, but then the magic was over. What happened to you and your wife? You want to pry into my life...let's turn the tables on you."

Adam froze. This wasn't a case of turning the tables...it was upending them. He struggled for the right words, wanting the pain that wrenched his gut to go away. "She died. And she was my fiancé. I never had the pleasure of marrying her before she was taken from me in a car accident. And that's the end of my story. Let's agree. Neither of us wants to talk about the past and leave well enough alone." His desire to help Erica had backfired.

She stiffened beside him but didn't say a word. The same sympathetic, not sure what to say, emotion hung in the air between them. "I'm sorry. I didn't realize. As to staying out of each other's lives...you have yourself a deal," she said, surprising him by not asking more questions. But then, given her situation, it made perfect sense.

Adam unloaded the suitcases, putting them in the living room. He placed the cane on the sofa nearby in case Erica needed it. Except Erica didn't seem to want to touch it, much less use the walking device. Which made next to no sense at all. "See you around," he said, waving as he left. She was right. They had nothing left to say. There had been too much time and life that happened over the years, making them into different people than the two young and naïve high school kids they once were.

Adam pulled out his phone, wanting to check in with Gilly, his right-hand man for the Wilderness Camp. Truth be told, his right arm, because without Gilly, the business would have gone under after Natalie died.

"What's up, boss?" Gilly answered, upbeat and chipper, as always.

"Not much. I'm just leaving town. Stopped to see an old friend, so it'll be a bit later before I can check the website and the bookings. Any trouble with today's guests on the trail ride?"

"Not a bit. They were repeats, which made the entire process easier. So, who's the old friend? Anyone I know?" Gilly asked, nosey as ever.

"Doubtful. You didn't grow up here." Adam laughed.

"Try me. What's his name?"

"Her name. Erica Carter."

"I see. Interesting."

"If you think it's interesting, you clearly don't see or understand the situation at all. She's just a friend. We used to be at camp together and I taught her to ride horses. Actually, *was a friend,* until I ruined it. Or more like her father did. Anyway, they were having a welcome home hero tribute for her in town, and I thought I should at least stop in to say hi."

"A hero, huh? This is getting more and more interesting. What did she do?" Gilly asked.

"Erica's not saying much, but I know there was an explosion, and she received a Purple Heart. She's very tightlipped about it all. I can tell something is really bothering her deep inside. She's not the same person she once was. I mean, she's dealing with physical injuries, but I think the emotional injuries are worse. And she's got those on lockdown."

"That's never good. Sorry to hear about your friend's troubles. Let me know if there's anything I can do to help," Gilly offered.

"I'll do what I can, but if Erica doesn't want help, then there's nothing I can do. Though I won't give up trying to get through to her." Adam owed it to Erica. They were once close friends, and friends were there for you when you needed them most.

"Maybe, maybe not. You never know what might happen that can change things."

Gilly was right. A little prayer and faith could go a long way. "True stuff. Glad today went well. I'll email you tonight with any schedule updates. Since you'll be gone three weeks on the next trail ride, make sure you put together a list of what you need for the next month's supply order so Mack can get the delivery set in motion while you're gone."

"Will do, boss." He'd told Gilly to stop calling him boss, but his friend wouldn't listen. Come to think of it, he didn't listen too much of anything if he disagreed. Which was one reason the two of them got along so well.

Chapter Three

❤

Sunlight streaming through the window had woken Erica from an exhausted sleep. She was thankful there had been no nightmares for the last five days since her return, but then the bed was downy soft and smelled of fresh flowers. It was like having her own personal aromatherapy treatment and perhaps another reason she slept so well.

Erica made her way down the stairs, pausing a second to listen to her aunt singing. Whenever she used to visit her aunt and uncle, they always went to church, and often, the praise team sang the Tim Hugh's song, *Here I am to Worship*. The words gave Erica a sense of peace. Something she didn't even realize she desperately needed after ten years of living in the barracks and traveling around the world on duty tours.

"Good morning, Aunt Mary," Erica said, joining her aunt in the kitchen.

"Good morning, dear. Did you sleep well?" Her aunt brushed back her gray curls from her face and adjusted her glasses.

Erica smiled. "Absolutely. I think it's the amazing aromatherapy treatment you're giving me on my pillow and sheets. I can't thank you enough for letting me stay here for a while to recover."

"I'm so glad you love spending time with us, and that you got another good night's rest. I'm worried about you. These past few days, you've been so quiet. Too quiet. And don't think you can hide the fact that you're in pain with your injuries. And I know you said you don't want to talk about it...but when you are ready...I'm a willing and sympathetic set of ears." Her aunt hugged her as she passed by on the way to the refrigerator.

Erica tried to relax, searching for the right words. "Thank you. I'm trying to forget what happened, not to keep reliving it. Military protocol demanded I repeat everything over and over until I started reliving the incident at night. I prefer not to discuss it, as I prefer to keep the nightmares at bay. These last few days have been a great start, and I want to hold on to the sweet peace of a good night's sleep for as long as I can."

"As you wish, dear. I wouldn't want to do anything that might cause you stress. If I had known, I would have tried harder to stop the party when it was first set in motion to welcome you to town."

"It's over and done. No worries. I'd rather figure out what I'm going to do next. I can't stay with you and Uncle John forever." Erica grinned as she poured a cup of coffee.

"Well, you could." Aunt Mary laughed. "Your uncle and I love having you here, but I also understand what you're saying. If there's anything we can do to help, please let us know. And don't feel you have to rush into any decisions. Take your time. Unwind. You just got here."

Erica nodded. "Thank you. I appreciate your generosity and love. You've always been there for me. Which is why I knew I needed to come back to Alaska." She took a sip of coffee, savoring the deep chicory flavor and the soothing warmth of the liquid.

"Thank you, dear. I'm fixing some farm fresh eggs and uncured bacon for breakfast. Healthy and full of protein to start the day. There's vegetable juice in the refrigerator if you'd like a glass. Breakfast should be ready in about ten minutes."

"Sounds lovely. Thank you." Erica moved to the kitchen table and sat down to wait. The less time on her feet, the better. Yesterday's fanfare arrival had taxed her physical limits with only an extra pain tablet to help her recover from the plantar fasciitis ache burning the bottoms of her feet. Walking weird after an injury had a way of throwing everything off kilter.

"Morning ladies," her uncle said as he entered the kitchen.

"Good morning," Erica said, smiling up at him. By the looks of his overalls, he was already hard at work. Knowing her uncle, probably since the crack of dawn.

"Good morning. Breakfast will be ready shortly, if that's why you're here," Aunt Mary said, kissing him on the cheek. After all these years, the two were still in love.

"I am hungry and would have shown up eventually, but I'm actually here now because the strangest thing just happened and I'm trying to put together the pieces. Erica, do you know anything about a special delivery?" His gaze landed on her, his brow furrowed.

"I only got here earlier this week. I haven't even had time to settle in yet, let alone figure out anything I need, so whatever it is, it's not mine." Her curiosity, however, was piqued based on her uncle's expression.

"Strange." Uncle John rubbed his chin and shook his head, clearly dumbfounded by something.

"What's going on, dear?" Aunt Mary asked.

Uncle John held up an envelope. "I was out in the barn and heard nothing, but when I came out, there was a black truck and horse trailer headed down the driveway. It took me a second to realize there was a mare tied up to one of the hitching posts."

"A horse? Why on earth would someone deliver a horse and then leave? Is it sickly? I reckon folks know we would help in any way we can, but we haven't had horses in quite some time now. And to drop the poor thing off, that's just wrong," Aunt Mary said, more than a little flustered with the turn of events.

"Hold on, you're jumping to conclusions. I didn't say it was sickly. Actually, it's a beautiful light chestnut quarter horse with a full-length white blaze marking down her nose. Her cream-colored mane is brushed and neat, her shoes appear to be professionally fit by a farrier or someone with extensive knowledge in the field, and the mare is well groomed. She stands about fifteen and a half hands high. Sweet disposition, from what I can tell. Honestly, she looks vaguely familiar, but I'm not sure why. There was a note attached to the halter, and the envelope is addressed to Erica."

Erica pulled back in surprise. "Me? Why would someone ever give me a horse? I don't even ride." Once upon a time she did, but no one knew about the passion she had developed for riding at camp. Something she hadn't done since then. Except there was one person who knew...Adam Landon. But why would he give her a horse?

"Maybe you should open the letter and find out." Uncle John shot a questioning frown at her aunt before handing Erica the envelope.

Curiosity far outweighed the fact she didn't want a horse and wasn't in any position to keep one. Even if she could ride. *Which she couldn't.* She slid open the envelope and pulled out the letter. Erica skimmed the page, more confused than ever. Moving back to the top, she read it out loud, knowing her aunt and uncle's curiosity was as great as her own.

Sundancer's Legacy

Sundancer was a legendary mare who helped Arabella, an early American pioneer woman, find peace and love with her new Indian family hundreds of years ago. Legend has it that the mare found Arabella after she had fallen sick and wandered off from her wagon train, which left her behind unknowingly. Finding Arabella near death, the mare led the warrior Tanveer to her. The brave warrior brought Arabella back to his teepee, and the women of the tribe nursed her back to health. Tanveer and Arabella fell in love, and he took her as his wife, giving her Sundancer as a wedding gift.

Over the years, Sundancer had many foals and Arabella gave them to other people based on two conditions. One, that all the descendant's first foals would bear the first name of Sundancer. And two, the first foal could never be sold, only gifted to someone with a broken spirit who needed help.

The legacy still lives on in the hearts of those helped, but also in the horses who bring the gift of hope and healing.

She finished reading and looked up at her aunt and uncle to gauge their reactions. "There's a PostScript at the end."

Sundancer's Joy is yours for as long as you want or need her. She can't be sold, only gifted to someone in need if you choose not to keep her. The same would go for her first foal. May Sundancer's Legacy bring you peace in your heart, and happiness in your life. It's time to rekindle your love for horses. Ride with the wind and be blessed.

"This is insane," Erica said, shocked at the enormity of the gift, but even more at the legacy that she had suddenly become a part of. Adam had to be the benefactor. Okay, so perhaps realistically, there were others who worked at the camp that would know. Still, this was beyond belief. "I don't ride. My foot..." she trailed off, unwilling to say the words. Without the full function of her leg and foot, it would be dangerous to ride...even if she wanted to...which she didn't. That was a part of her life she didn't want to relive. Especially given it hadn't ended well.

The horse had to go back to wherever she came from, and Erica's best bet was to start with Adam. If it wasn't him, she would talk to some folks in town and discover who used to own Sundancer's Joy.

"While it's true, it's an extravagant gift, I see no reason you can't learn to ride. I could adjust the stirrup for you, no problem," her uncle offered, jumping to the conclusion she should keep the horse.

"No. I'm not a charity case and I don't want a horse, and I don't want to learn to ride. I just want to be left alone," Erica huffed, and stood, limping toward the kitchen door. "Sorry, Aunt Mary, I've lost my appetite." She desperately needed to get some fresh air.

"Don't worry, dear. You take whatever time you need. I'll keep some leftovers for you in case you change your mind," Aunt Mary said, a concerned expression etched on her face.

"Well, well. What do you make of all this?" Erica heard her uncle's question as the door closed behind her.

She should have stayed to hear the answer, but the need to get outside consumed Erica. After grabbing her parka and gloves, she headed out the front door. It was no surprise that her path led straight to the barn. Her foot protested her fast pace, but Erica was determined to see the horse. *Sundancer's Joy*. There wasn't room for joy in her life at the moment, the horse or the emotion.

As she neared the barn, Erica spotted the mare. Sleek and beautiful, exactly as her uncle had described the horse. The white blaze patch down her nose made her appear distinct, regal in fact, as the white fanned out across to the eyes. Joy watched Erica's approach with great interest.

"Hey, girl. You are beautiful." Erica reached up and stroked the mare's nose and scratched behind her ears. It wasn't the mare's fault someone had given her to the wrong person. Joy nudged her head against Erica's head softly. It was as though the horse was instantly bonding with her. But why? Could there be any truth to the legacy? Did these horses sense when someone was lost in a sea of emotional baggage?

Erica didn't want to believe it. Either way, the horse had to go. When she removed her hand, the intensity of the bond lessened but didn't vanish.

She reached out again and smoothed back Joy's sleek, cream-colored mane.

Yes, it was definitely different, as though through touch, the two of them connected. "I wish things were different. I hope you understand. This isn't a good time for me. Not to mention I don't know how to ride anymore." Erica leaned her head forward and rested against Joy's neck, inhaling the fresh scent of the horse and loving it. It was the same sense of peace she felt this morning, only stronger.

Images from the past, riding through the meadows with Adam, assailed her. She shook her head, trying to dispel the memory, untied Joy, and led her into the barn. Until Erica found out where the horse had come from and returned Joy to the benefactor, it was up to her to take care of the mare.

And in her quest to find Joy's owner, she'd start by talking to the most likely source. Adam. She hadn't heard from him at all in the past few days, which, no matter how hard she tried, hurt. Just a little, but to her way of thinking, any amount was unsettling. Erica pulled out her phone and searched for his number, intent on getting an answer one way or the other, so she knew her next move.

Erica: Question. Did you have anything to do with the chestnut mare that showed up at our barn this morning?

Being direct had always been her preference.

Her phone pinged a minute later.

Adam: Good morning to you too. What mare?

Erica: Good morning. Sorry, things have been a little hectic here with the surprise delivery of a horse. To me.

Adam: Interesting, but I don't know a thing about it. Hope your day gets better. Let me know if there's anything I can do to help.

Enough chit chat. She'd been wrong about Adam, which would have been the easiest answer. Instead, she would need to go into town, where more people would look at her with sympathetic and curious gazes. But it was the only way she would find out who owned Joy, and when her aunt offered to drive, Erica was more than happy to accept.

Quickly changing into jeans and a T-shirt, she headed downstairs.

"Ready, dear?" her aunt asked.

"For sure. Perhaps we could start at Kodiak's hardware store and then head over to the Glacier Grill. Mr. Thompson and Mattie were always so nice to me when I was younger." Erica followed her aunt to the car, preferring to stay behind people in order to avoid them having to watch her painful attempts at walking.

"Are you sure you want to give up the mare? Your uncle seems to think she is a very special horse, and it might be good for you to take up riding. It would certainly give you something to do. Not to mention, think of the fresh air and exercise."

All valid points, but none that would change the outcome. It was Erica's decision, and she disagreed. She knew her aunt and uncle were trying to help in any way they could. Except they didn't know the whole story, and it was better this way.

It wasn't long before Aunt Mary parked in front of Kodiak's. "Do you want me to go in with you?"

"No, thank you. I can handle my own inquiries." Erica laughed.

"Okay. I'll wait here. Good luck."

Erica headed inside, the overhead bell jingling. She stopped, scanning the visible aisles in in search of Mr. Thompson.

"Well, hello, Erica. What brings you out this way so early? Starting a project already?" Harvey asked, grinning. The old man had run the store for the past fifty years and was a lot slower when he moved.

"No projects, Mr. Thompson. I came for information and since you know everyone in town, I figured you were the best place to start."

He nodded. "I'll try to help you if I can. What is it you want to know?" he asked, pushing his glasses up on his nose to see her better.

"A horse was delivered to me this morning as a gift. Ever heard of the Sundancer Legacy?"

"I've heard it mentioned a few times over the years. Something about hope and healing, right?"

"Yes, and you got it on the first try. Do you know who owns Sundancer's Joy?"

Harvey frowned, his silence magnified by the ticking of the grandfather clock on the wall behind him. Perhaps he was simply trying to remember. "Well, I reckon if the mare was a gift, you would be the new owner."

"No. I need to know who owned the mare before this morning. It's important that I find out who delivered her."

"Seems to me if the giver wanted to be known, you would already know. Why do you want to know?"

"To give her back, of course."

His brow furrowed, the deep lines like a plowed cornfield. "I see," he said, without further comment.

"Do you know who owned her?" she repeated, wondering if he forgot the question.

Harvey stroked his chin as though deep in thought. "I seem to recall a man by the name of Zeke Haskins was connected with the mare. Lives close to Turner Lake in a place called Kigiktok. They say he received a legacy horse a long time ago. Probably could ask him."

Erica had never heard of either place. "How do I get there?" she pressed.

"Now that's another problem all of its own. Kigiktok is a day and half ride from here, and involves crossing the Taku River just past the inlet, up around Folly's Gulch."

Now they were getting somewhere. "Thanks for all the good information. But I'll need a few more details if I'm going to drive out to this guy's place with the horse trailer."

Harvey shook his head. "Not that kind of ride. It's a trail ride into Alaska's rugged wilderness. Zeke's got a remote lodge not far from the edge of the Taku glacier. Folks hike, trail ride, or catch a flight in a seaplane to the nearby lake to get there. He's only open a few months out of the year. Beautiful country though."

A trail ride was not at all what she had in mind. Especially since she was more than a little rusty at her riding skills. "I wouldn't know the first thing about how to get to such a remote location. What would you suggest?" There was also the little matter that Erica wasn't even sure she could ride again, not with her injury. But there was no sense in bringing up the complication in the conversation with Harvey, given it would more than likely lead to questions she didn't want to answer.

"Adam Landon is the best wilderness guide there is in this area. Seems to me he'd be your best bet. I'm sure he knows Zeke."

It didn't seem like she could escape Adam. "I see." *Seeing didn't mean she had to like it.*

"You could just keep the horse. Must be pretty special if it's a legacy horse."

"She's beautiful and gentle and has these all-knowing eyes that watch me. Unfortunately, I can't keep a horse and the huge responsibilities that come with one."

"I see," he said, copying her earlier comment.

"Thanks for your help," Erica said, waving as she hobbled out the door. She could only hope folks at the Glacier Grill had better and completely different information. She made her way across the street and headed inside.

Ten minutes later, she left the diner and headed for the car where her aunt waited. Erica couldn't believe it. The answers she got mirrored what Harvey said, or close enough anyway. There were a few alternative suggestions to Adam, but they all insisted he was the number one guide in the area. It would seem she needed to enlist Adam's aid if she wanted to return Joy to the man who lived in Kigiktok. The man everyone seemed to think might have owned the horse.

Chapter Four

♥

Adam turned off the coffee maker and emptied his now cold cup of morning brew into the sink and headed for the door. Erica's text messages about someone gifting her a mare had thrown him for a loop. It was a brilliant idea, one he wished he'd thought of first. She loved to ride when they were at camp and perhaps it was just what she needed to help her now. Unfortunately, the horse she should have been given was stabled at the wilderness camp in Takuwok with Gilly.

Shortly after her texts, Harriet, the town council secretary, called, and he spent the next hour arguing the validity of the Sidekick Squad Connection. It would seem Natalie's mother, Maureen, was up to her old tricks again to stop the program.

When Adam hung up, he was more than a little frustrated and irritated with Maureen, and the entire town council, for that matter. He was already behind schedule for the day, and now he needed to attend another special town council meeting. They would vote on the uniqueness quality of the Sidekick Squad Connection to decide if it was different enough from other non-profits in the surrounding areas of the state. A vague requirement for new non-profit organizations that Maureen managed to dig up.

The program *was* different. Natalie had seen to that in her precise, detailed planning. But now, it was up to him to prove it. He was sure Maureen was gloating at the moment, as her efforts to stop him seemed to have found some traction. Obviously, she didn't know Adam well enough to realize he would never give up. *Not until he made Natalie's dream come true.*

Adam was a patient man. For more than a year, Maureen had been a thorn in his side. He totally understood she was grieving for her daughter, but he couldn't understand her need to put an end to something that Natalie had dedicated the last couple of years of her life to make happen.

So many children, and for that matter, adults, would benefit from the Christian program that would help kids with a positive growth journey into adulthood. Adam thought everything was in place, and the grand opening was just over a month away. But he should have known Maureen wouldn't give up. She played bridge on Monday nights with Valerie Jenkins, the vice-president of the town council, which gave her an edge in swaying the council's decisions.

Adam grabbed his wallet and keys off the counter and then pulled on his heavy boots and parka. He braced himself for the chill as he opened the door and was more than a little shocked to discover Erica standing there, poised to knock. "Well, hello. What a nice surprise."

Erica's hand dropped, and she took a step back. "Hello to you too. I'm so glad you're here. I sensed that you still spend a lot of time at the cabin in the woods, but I was hoping you hadn't gone back yet."

Adam shook his head. "Oh, no. I'm here until the Sidekick Squad has its grand opening."

Erica adjusted her head, pulling her hat lower over her ears. "Isn't it a voluntary program? Why has it taken you so long?" Erica asked.

"It's a non-profit organization, and you'd be surprised. Especially when it comes to funding and bureaucratic red tape. What brings you out my way?"

Suddenly she was all business, the lines across her forehead deepening. "I've got a problem. And it would seem folks in town think you are the best person to help me."

Adam frowned. "I'm lost. What do you mean?"

"Do you remember when I told you about the horse someone dropped off this morning?"

"Of course, it wasn't that long ago."

"Well, since you weren't the benefactor, I talked to Harry at the hardware store and Mattie at the Glacier Grill about the horse. They seem to think some guy named Zeke Haskins in Kigiktok would be a good person to ask, as they seem to remember he, too, was given a special horse many years ago when his wife and son died."

Adam's gaze intensified, the direction of the conversation having taken an interesting and strange twist. He'd met Zeke Haskins a few times, but hadn't been out to Kigiktok in over five years. "You love horses, so what's the problem with this one?"

"I don't ride and don't want the responsibility of a horse. I can barely walk some days. I don't even know what I'm going to do with my life at the moment." Erica let out a deep breath, as though the explanation cost her. "And why would someone give me a horse anyway when no one knows I used to ride?" Erica asked.

Adam shrugged. "Someone knows."

"Exactly. It's why I thought of you initially," she said.

"Fair. So why do you want to visit Zeke? There's no easy way to get there."

"So I've heard, which is where you come in. I want to return the horse to Zeke. He seems the most likely person, given the information I've received."

"The horse was a gift. Why not accept that? And it's easy enough to relearn how to ride. Let the horse be your legs." The more he thought about it, the more he realized a horse was perfect for Erica.

"No, I'm not interested. And that's the end of it, or it will be as soon as I can get rid of the horse.

The mare has to go back to the owner because the legacy note says I can't sell her, only keep her or give her to someone else in need. I don't need charity from someone, and the doctors have already seen to my healing, or at least the best they can do for me. I'm sure there are a lot of people more deserving of such a special horse."

Adam blanched. *Legacy horse*. This didn't make any sense. Sundancer's Joy was the only legacy horse in the area that he knew of. *Find someone that needs her.* The words he uttered to Gilly several months ago echoed in his head. It couldn't be. Gilly wouldn't...would he? "What's the horse's name?"

"Sundancer's Joy."

Adam jerked back, stunned by the confirmation of information he only suspected. It was the perfect horse for Erica and if he told her everything he knew, Joy would be in his barn within the hour. "Beautiful name," he said, stumbling over the words as he tried to regroup from the revelation.

"Beautiful horse. And so sweet...but not mine." Erica almost sounded disappointed, which was all the more reason for him to keep silent about Gilly's gift.

"That remains to be seen. You know, healing isn't always on the outside. And you have your share of issues with whatever happened in Afghanistan. You keep it bottled inside and it will eat you alive one day at a time. Perhaps you should reconsider such an incredible gift."

Erica shook her head. "I've given it a lot of thought, but I can't."

"Isn't that where the expression 'looking a gift horse in the mouth' comes from?" he asked, trying to change her mind.

"It doesn't matter. Will you help me learn to ride again and then take me to Kigiktok? I'd just call the guy and ask, but they tell me there's no internet or cell service in that part of the back-country."

Spending time with Erica wasn't a good idea, and there just wasn't enough time in his schedule. And pointing her in Gilly's direction would be a mistake. Luckily, he was headed out on a trail ride tomorrow morning and would be gone for a week. "As much as I would love to help, I've got the final fundraiser for the program coming up in less than a week at my place, and it's all I can do to stay ahead of Maureen Vincent. In fact, I've got to get to the town hall now for an impromptu council meeting." Her downcast look was almost his undoing, but the Sidekick Squad was his priority.

"It's only a day to help me learn to ride again, and I'm told it's only a few days out and back. They say you're the best guide in this part of Alaska. Surely you can spare a few days. Please," she asked, her voice borderline desperate.

Adam swallowed hard, fighting back against the urge to say yes. "I'm sorry, the answer is still no."

Erica frowned, the lines on her forehead growing deeper with her frustration. "I can't believe you won't help me. What am I supposed to do with the horse in the meantime?"

The same thing Adam had done once upon a time. "Keep her. Seems like a welcome-home gift if you ask me. Perhaps you should give the horse a chance?" It would be the best course of action for Erica. Gilly was a genius, as long as it didn't get Adam in hot water with her. He remembered all too well that Erica was full of stubborn pride, and she didn't enjoy coming up against a brick wall. Erica wouldn't want his sympathy. *Far from it.* It would make her feel weak, something she could never abide. Which was why she could never find out that although Gilly had gifted her Joy, his friend was acting on Adam's behalf.

Erica stepped off the porch, but then turned back. "Not going to happen. So, why is this Maureen woman determined to stop you from launching the program?"

"She's Natalie's mother. The woman is blinded by grief and refuses to see this as a tribute to her daughter. Natalie died in a car accident while attending a Sidekick Squad Connection meeting. It was her dream to see the program come to life, matching children and mentors. Her passion was to help children who needed a better adult influence in their life with adults who wanted to make a difference. Natalie gave everything she had to make this dream a reality and I won't stop until I've realized the dream for her. With or without her mother on board."

Erica nodded. "That's a shame. Well, I guess I'll see you around, cowboy." She turned and headed for the car, her limp and slow pace a dead giveaway to the pain she was experiencing.

The memory of the past flooded Adam. He had been in a terrible place after Natalie died, and he had holed up at the wilderness camp to avoid all the sympathy and pity that came with sticking around in town. A few days after he arrived, Gilly left on a guided trip with a large group, taking all the horses, including Adam's trail horse. It was a three-week trek into the rugged backcountry of Alaska, leaving Adam to the solitude he craved.

Shortly after that, Sundancer's Joy had shown up, complete with the legacy letter. Adam had been forced to take care of the mare with no one else around. It was a slow process, but Sundancer's Joy had been just what he needed to pull him back into reality and dig his way out of the darkness that had clouded his world. And now, if Erica would give the horse a chance, Adam was certain that Joy could do the same for her.

It came as quite a pleasant surprise that no one disclosed Adam's identity as Joy's previous owner. They knew about the legacy, and that he'd been an unwilling benefactor eighteen months ago. And it would seem the folks in town were still protecting him.

Either that or they were matchmaking.

Something that would never happen. They didn't know the history between him and Erica, and more importantly, though he'd been healed emotionally as best he could...Adam would always love Natalie.

His heart was closed to love.

Forever.

Chapter Five

♥

Erica returned home, the conversation with Adam playing over and over in her head. The love in his voice for Natalie was as obvious as the moon on a clear summer's eve. Bright and shining, and full of awe and wonder. His fiancé had been a lucky woman to have the devoted love of an amazing man. She shook her head, trying to clear her thoughts. It wouldn't do any good to dwell on the past or current state of Adam's heart and emotions.

Pulling into the driveway, she passed the barn and continued to the house, parking in front. Reaching for the door, she paused before getting out. What she wanted to do was head for the barn, the urge strong enough she couldn't deny the need to see Joy. It wasn't the horse's fault that Erica wasn't up to keeping her or taking care of her the way she deserved. A legacy horse. A mare born to ride like the wind and give healing to others.

Adam seemed to believe riding horseback was an art you never forgot. She hoped he was right, because as luck would have it, or unlucky, as the case may be, she would have to ride a horse again to return Joy.

Did she dare risk it given everything, given the slow and painful healing process she'd already been through? She could find a new recipient, but that might take a long time. Time she didn't have.

Erica still couldn't believe Adam refused to help her. It was the second time in her life he let her down. Though why he showed up at the welcome party was beyond her. She was being uncharitable and hated knowing the truth. The fundraiser was important, and it was selfish of her to demand otherwise. People were counting on Adam and the program, and she didn't want to be the one to ruin such a wonderful opportunity for the kids. Adam, it would seem, was an honorable man, and not at all the picture she had painted in her head for years.

Decision made; Erica headed for the barn. Bits and pieces of conversation with folks in town came to mind. Everyone seemed to think Adam was the man for the job of helping her find Zeke, and not once had she...or anyone else considered he would turn her down. They had also mentioned Adam's assistant, Gilly. Then there was some guy by the name of Ralph Thorton, who came recommended but with some reservations.

There was not much to choose from, and she would have preferred not to ride off into who knows where with a stranger, but she would do what had to be done. Erica didn't like to back down from a challenge, and this was a doozy.

Well, if Adam wouldn't go with her, his second in command at the Wilderness Camp was an easy second choice. She pulled out her phone and searched for the phone number of the Wilderness Camp in Takuwok. Erica dialed the number and waited, trying to figure out what to say to the guy.

"Wilderness Camp Trail Guides, this is Gilly."

"Hi Gilly. My name is Erica Carter, and I'm looking to hire a trail guide for a few days to take me up to Kigiktok."

"Did you say Erica Carter?"

"Yes, why?"

"You must be Adam's friend."

Friend was a strong word for what they shared. "I'm not sure you can call us friends, but we know each other for sure."

"Cool. Nice talking to you. So when are you looking to do this trail ride? I'm fairly booked up for the foreseeable future."

"Oh. I didn't think of that. I was hoping we could go right away. Day after tomorrow?"

"No can do. Sorry. The earliest I can squeeze in that run would be like the middle of May. Will that work?"

"No, but thanks. I appreciate your time." *All three minutes of it.* She hadn't considered that in Alaska, trail guides would be in high demand and booked months in advance.

"No worries. If you change your mind, give me a holler. I'd really like to help you out since you know the boss. Maybe you could talk him into taking you."

"Already tried, but he's busy with the Sidekick Squad. But thanks for the thought. Bye now."

"Have a good day," Gilly said, before the call disconnected.

Strike two.

Based on what Gilly told her, there wasn't much chance of the third guy being available either. Although his recommendations weren't as rock solid as the first two, they were still worth a shot. She wasn't giving up that easily.

Decision made, Erica turned around, making her way to the car. She drove to town and pulled up in front of the Golden Nugget, the place where Mattie, the owner of the Glacier Grill, mentioned Ralph frequented. It was her best bet to confront the man personally, with the added benefit of being able to size him up for herself when it came to the sanity of riding off into the wilderness with the guy.

Erica pushed open the door to the Golden Nugget and walked in. Glancing around, she spotted the bartender and made her way over to the bar. The lingering odor of smoke and alcohol stung her throat and eyes as she waited for the petite woman to acknowledge her.

The woman's purple and green hair was pulled back into a ponytail. Her fingernails were coated in black polish, and her fingers were covered with silver rings that sparkled in the light. Old enough to tend bar, but probably not a day over twenty-two.

"What can I get you?" the woman asked, sliding a napkin in her direction.

"Sorry, I don't need a drink. I was hoping to find a man by the name of Ralph Thorton. Do you know if he's here?"

The woman frowned, intently inspecting Erica. "Who are you? And what do you want with him? We don't take kindly to strangers poking their nose into other people's business."

Erica hadn't considered an introduction to the guy would be a problem. More so, that he would actually need protection from strangers. What did that say about Mr. Thorton? "I'm not the law, if that's what you're asking. I'm Erica Carter. I just arrived back in town and find myself in need of a guide. Someone offered up Ralph's name as a possibility, and the other two guys I spoke with aren't available."

The woman continued to stare at her, the seconds slowly ticking by. She finally relaxed, as though satisfied with her assessment. "Guessing you must be the military chick the whole town's talking about this past week."

Erica nodded. "It would seem that way." *Not that she liked or wanted it.*

"I'm surprised Adam wouldn't take the job, seeing as he has a company to run. But none of my business. Ralph's over there," the woman said, jerking her thumb toward a corner booth. The guy was drinking a beer, a woman draped all over him as though he was sweeter than apple pie. *Highly unlikely.*

"Thanks." The bartender moved off to help someone else.

Erica headed for the table. "Ralph Thorton?" she asked when he looked up at her, a gleam of interest in his eyes. *Not a chance, mister.*

"That's me. Whatever you want, it's yours." He grinned. "A pretty new face in town is always a highlight."

The woman with him frowned. "I thought you were happy to see me?" she crooned, a slight tinny whine to her voice.

"I am, darling. But why don't you go get yourself a drink and let me find out what the lady needs." The blonde seemed confused but was instantly mollified when Ralph dropped a twenty-dollar bill in her hand to pay for the drinks.

Ralph turned back to her. "So, what's up, darling?"

Strictly business meant eliminating all chances for misdirection of intentions. "I'm not your darling, but I do want to hire your services. As a guide," she added, not willing to give the guy any room for misinterpreting.

One eyebrow quirked crookedly, his sudden surprised interest all too obvious. "And exactly where are you looking to go?"

"Kigiktok. I need to meet up with Zeke Haskins. My sources say there's no cell service that far out in the wilderness. I'm also told you can help me."

His face twisted in disdain. "In other words, Adam and Gilly said no."

"How...never mind. I've got a horse I'm looking to return to Zeke if he's the rightful owner."

"You do realize that means we would need to take along a third horse, unless you intend to stay there. And how did you come into possession of this horse, and why do you want to get rid of it?" He took a swig of his drink and leveled her with a questioning glint in his eyes that wanted answers.

Erica sat down across from Ralph, glancing at the woman waiting for her drinks at the bar. She filled Ralph in on the details, the man not giving a clue what he was thinking. His answering grin gave her hope she'd found herself a guide.

"I'm in. Can't leave a pretty lady like yourself traipsing through the wilderness. More than likely, you wouldn't find your way back or you would be eaten by grizzly bears." Ralph chuckled.

This was an aspect of the journey she hadn't even considered. The dangers associated with a trek into the Alaskan wilderness were not for the faint of heart. "Will they attack us?"

Ralph shook his head. "Doubt it, but I can't make any promises. It'll cost you two thousand dollars for three days of my time. Includes food rations, supplies, and the cost for the extra horse we'll need for your return trip." He leaned back, his study of her unnerving.

"Two thousand dollars? That's a lot of money," she squeaked. This was something else she hadn't counted on with her plan to return the horse.

His grin deepened. "Well, doesn't sound like you have much choice if you want to go to Kigik-tok. Take it or leave it."

Erica let out a deep breath. Keeping a horse would be even more expensive...eventually. "You have a deal. When do we leave? I can be ready first thing in the morning." Not that she knew how to ride, but Ralph would have to help her relearn. At least she would get something extra for the money.

"*Whoa*. Not so fast. I've got a few things I need to take care of before I can leave, and there is some planning and packing required for the trip."

He had a point, and unfortunately, there was nothing she could do about the delay. "Fine. Reckon I don't have much choice."

"You don't," he said, glancing up as the woman approached with their drinks. "Now, if you don't mind, I'm on a date and would like to get back to the business of having fun."

Erica stood, allowing the woman to settle back in her place. "Everything okay, darling?"

"Peachy. Seems I'm going on a camping trip with the pretty lady for a few days."

The woman's scowl deepened. "Can I come along? I want to stay with you," she whined.

"Not a chance. Doubt you're the outdoorsy type anyway." He glanced up at Erica. "Meet me here Saturday morning, eight AM."

Erica wanted to argue Saturday was four days away, but understood all too well Ralph wouldn't budge. He held all the cards for this trip. The guy seemed nice enough, just full of himself. Which could be a good quality in a guide she was trusting to lead her into the wilderness to some off the grid location and then get back to Juneau.

Safely.

Chapter Six

♥

The buzz of conversation swirled around Adam as he ate the humongous western burrito Mattie was famous for serving at the Glacier Grill. He tried to block it all out and was mostly successful. Except for the kid climbing across the back of his seat and poking his shoulder. At least the boy's hands weren't covered in maple syrup. Adam polished off the rest of his coffee and slid the mug across the table. Picking up the tab, he tossed a five-dollar bill on the table, slid out of the booth, and headed for the checkout register.

A quick breakfast was all he could handle, otherwise, sitting still left him way too much thinking time. Thoughts of Natalie. And Erica. Thoughts that left him feeling guilty. His fiancé died over a year and a half ago, but what they had shared and the future they might have shared were never far from mind. *At least not until Erica showed up in town.*

Which is where the confusion came in. He hadn't been prepared for old feelings to resurface. Feelings he didn't want to acknowledge. *Or want.*

He handed the tab to Mattie.

"How's the fundraiser coming along? Do you think the program will start soon?" she asked. Not only was Mattie the owner of Glacier Grill, but she was also an integral part of the town council, having been the president for the last twenty years. Mattie talked and others listened.

"I think everything is moving along. Tamila has been an absolute gem in planning the event. Couldn't have done it without her organizational skills. Now, there's just a few loose ends to clean up. I'll be glad when this is over, and we can finally start helping the children."

"Sidekick Squad Connection is a wonderful idea, and you know I support you one hundred percent. In fact, I signed up to be a mentor. Unfortunately, I have to play by the rules and follow protocol when Maureen starts down her self-destructive path. One day, she'll see the light and thank you for honoring Natalie with such a special tribute."

"Let's just hope you're right. And thanks for your support. The whole town it seems, loves the idea...except Natalie's mother." Adam let out a deep sigh.

"What's this I hear about Erica Carter going off into the wilderness with Ralph? It came as quite a surprise considering you're the top guide in town, and a whole lot more trustworthy."

"Ralph Thorton?" he asked, praying he was mistaken.

Mattie's gaze held more than a hint of accusation. "Well, we only have three wilderness guides in the area. What did you expect her to do when you said no?"

Adam flinched. "She should know better. Of all the foolhardy—"

"She's a headstrong girl. Just like her mother, Laura. I was still surprised when they left town and got divorced though. Anyhow, it's mighty interesting you turned down helping Erica find Sundancer Joy's benefactor, seeing as we both know who the rightful owner is. What game are you playing, Adam?" Mattie was headstrong too, and outspoken to match.

"No game. Once upon a time, Erica and I were friends at the camp in high school. The woman who came home from Afghanistan is not the real Erica, at least not on the inside. She was a free spirit who laughed and lived wholeheartedly. I didn't give the mare to Erica, Gilly did. I had told him a bit about Erica, and he took it upon himself to gift Joy to her. A couple of months ago, I tasked him with finding Joy a new owner, someone that needed hope and healing to honor the legacy. I think he made an excellent choice. Joy can help Erica, I just know it. The legacy hasn't failed yet...look at me."

Mattie ran a hand through her silvery white hair and shook her head. "I am looking at you, Adam. What I see is someone who has an altruistic motive for keeping quiet, but lacks follow through on the implementation plan. You can't let her go on a fool's errand alone, especially with the likes of Ralph. Besides, you and I both know this will never end well for you when Erica learns the truth."

"Let's just hope by then she's found inner peace and joy for herself. Her anger at me would be well worth her healing." But the idea of Ralph taking her into the wilderness brought him zero peace or joy. He had to stop her.

"I see. Sounds to me like you still have feelings for her. Perhaps you were more than friends in high school," Mattie said, her voice dropping a notch or two. She was grasping at information he didn't plan to provide.

"Hardly. Natalie…" he trailed off, unwilling to say the words.

"Isn't here. It's been a year and a half and it's time you started living again outside of putting together her program. It's time to let go, Adam." The logical side of him agreed with Mattie, but where his heart was concerned, that part of his life would always belong to Natalie. "Not a chance."

The lines on her forehead deepened as she stood there, hands on hips. "And you're really going to let Erica go off alone into the wilderness with Ralph?"

"Not a chance."

Mattie patted his hand affectionately. "That a boy. I always knew you were a smart one. Now run along and find Erica and let her know you've changed your mind...before they leave town. This one's on me," she added, tearing up the tab.

"Thanks, Mattie. And for the record, I thought Erica would simply keep the horse. If that happened, I figured it would give them time to bond and everything would turn out as it should. I've got to stop Erica from making this mistake." Adam waved as he left, unwilling to dwell on why it was so important, but his gut told him he was the man for the job. If Erica wanted to visit Zeke, he would be the one taking her. Erica was far too vulnerable right now, and it was up to him to protect her.

For old times' sake. Especially given he was the one who broke her heart in high school without so much as a word. Not that he didn't have a reason. Erica's father had given him plenty. Not to mention, faith and integrity came into play, and he chose to respect her father's wishes.

Adam headed for the Carter's ranch, hoping to catch Erica. He pulled up in front of the house and noticed Mary rocking on the porch. Sliding out of the truck, he took the steps two at a time. "Morning. Erica around by any chance?" he asked, unable to keep the sense of urgency out of his voice.

Mary rose to greet him, the woman quite imposing at almost six feet tall. Normally a smile at the ready, her stern expression caught him off guard. "I was hoping you'd come by. Either that, or I was going to have to hunt you down for some answers. Erica's gone into town to buy a few things for her trip into the wilderness. A trip she shouldn't be taking, and we both know it. Mind telling me what's going on, young man? I've not said a word out of respect for you and all you've been through when you lost Natalie. But you better have a good reason for withholding information from Erica, because I'm not sure I can let her go on this trek with the likes of Ralph Thorton."

"I understand, and I'm grateful for the silence. The problem is we both know if she finds out the horse is mine, she will drop Joy at my place and be done with the whole situation. Something we can't let happen because Erica needs a connection to life again. She's subdued and quiet, which is so unlike her. I'm hoping Joy will bring her the same sense of hope and healing I got from the mare. Erica needs help, but she's too stubborn to ask anyone. Gilly gifted her the horse on my behalf without me knowing. I told him to find a new owner, but I swear I didn't know about him giving Joy to Erica until this morning. She loves horses, and Joy is special...but they need time together for this to happen." He wasn't sure if he was trying to convince Mary...or himself.

Mary stepped closer, closing the distance between them. "And for her to spend time with Joy, you're proposing she go off alone with Ralph to find Zeke? Sounds like a fool's errand, if you ask me," she huffed.

"Hardly. I figured Erica wouldn't go, and then once she spent time with Joy, all would end well. Clearly, I thought wrong. I'm here to stop her from going with Ralph and plan to take her to Zeke's myself."

Mary let out a sigh of relief. "What changed? I heard you told her no, which is why I was so upset with the whole mess."

"Ralph changed everything. We both know he's not trustworthy enough to take care of Erica, especially with everything else she's dealing with at the moment. And I'm sure folks told her to call Gilly, but he's leaving shortly for a three-week trip.

Erica's always been strong, but I feel like she's on the verge of breaking. I'll deal with the fallout if Erica learns the truth. Hopefully, by then she'll have bonded with Joy."

"So how is it you know Erica? Well enough that she was comfortable leaving the party with you," Mary asked.

"We were friends," Adam said, looking away.

"Whatever you say. This has the look and feel of so much more, but I'll leave you two to figure that out. Maybe there's more healing in store for you as well, Adam. I'll let this farce continue, but only if you promise to take care of Erica and return her home safely. We agree with you about Joy and pray the horse can bring healing...but no monkey business. Do you hear me?"

Adam nodded. "You have my word."

"Now all you have to do is convince her you made a mistake and cancel her plans with Ralph. She was pretty upset when you said no."

"Like I told Erica, I really can't afford to take time off this close to the final fundraiser with so much riding on the line, but Erica is important too. I just need to get to Zeke's and back in time for the event, which means we have a tight schedule to make this happen. No time for dillydallying. Hopefully, my assistant can handle everything, and we won't have any more obstacles popping up, courtesy of Maureen Vincent."

She placed a hand on his arm. "Sounds like you have it all worked out. Good luck, Adam. Truly. With everything."

"Thanks for your support, Mary. It means a lot to me."

A swirl of dust was visible in the distance as a car approached the house.

"You both deserve it. Looks like Erica's back, so I'll leave you to it. It'll take some sweet talking, I'm sure." Mary shot him a wink before heading inside the house.

Adam leaned against the porch post, waiting for Erica to recognize him. Her movements were slow and methodical as she retrieved a few bags from the back seat. He moved forward to offer assistance. "Let me help you with these," he said, catching her off guard, judging by the sudden jerk as she swung around and faced him.

"You? What are you doing here?"

Not one to be put off, Adam jumped right in. "Well, hello to you, too. I've come to offer my help."

Erica frowned. "To carry in my bags? Seems a long way to drive out here for such a simple task."

"No, to offer to take you to meet up with Zeke."

Her guarded expression slipped to one of surprise before she turned away. "You're too late. I already have another guide."

"That's what I heard. Clearly, you don't know Ralph well enough, or you wouldn't have even asked him. He's a hard one to trust."

"Like you're any better. I seem to remember you pulling a disappearing act all those years ago. You told me one thing and did something completely different."

They were back to this, but he still wouldn't offer the truth. It was history, and maligning her father's character would serve no purpose. "I had my reasons."

"So you've said. The answer is no," she snapped. "Now, if you don't mind, I've got to pack."

"Erica, stop being bull-headed. You know as well as I do that you'll be safer with me. It can be tricky getting around the river this time of year, but I grew up in that area if you recall."

"What's changed? You were too busy for me yesterday."

"Let's just say I moved some things around in my schedule to make it happen. If it's important to you, it's important to me. The only condition is that we get to Zeke's, and whether or not he's the owner, we come straight back here. I can't miss the fundraiser. I've worked hard to make this happen for a year and a half. Surely you understand."

Erica let out a deep breath. Her hesitation worried him. "How much?"

"How much what?" he asked, confused by the sudden change in conversation.

"How much do you charge for your services?"

"Free."

"I'm not looking for your charity."

"It's not charity. We are friends. This is a chance for me to make the past up to you, and it would be great if you could forgive me."

"Well, I didn't relish draining my savings account to return a horse I don't want. Ralph is charging me two thousand dollars, so I reckon you have yourself a deal. I want to leave first thing in the morning. Six AM. Pick me up here, and don't forget you need a second horse. I'll not be riding double with you on the return trip."

Adam let out a deep breath, relieved when she said yes. Early in the morning would give them a little extra time, which worked perfectly for him. "Deal. And thanks, Erica." The extra horse was unnecessary, but he couldn't exactly explain why without giving away the truth. It would slow them down, but he could make it work if they followed Herbert River and cut across at Indian Cove.

"For what?"

"Trusting me."

Erica nodded and then headed up the steps without another word, the door closing solidly behind her as she disappeared into the house. Her limp was more pronounced than he remembered it. Most likely from overdoing it as she prepared for the trip. Another reason for him to feel guilty. Adam made it to his truck when he heard his name being called. He swung back around, surprised to see Erica.

"There's only one small problem with leaving in the morning," she called out.

Her hesitation warmed his heart as she shifted her weight, rocking from side to side, her arms protectively folded around her waist. A quick glimpse in his direction before focusing on a flowering plant hanging from the porch was almost his undoing.

It was this lack of self-confidence Adam hated to see. "I'm sure whatever it is, we can fix it."

"You're forgetting, I don't remember how to ride. I was going to wing it with Ralph, but I don't want to look like a complete fool in front of you, so you may as well know the truth."

"It's like riding a bike...you were a natural as a kid. Just believe in yourself."

"Easier said than done. Any chance you want to give me a lesson? Now. You taught me before and—"

"Consider it done." Adam slammed the truck door shut and closed the distance between them. "We can saddle Joy and run through some basics in a paddock. Enough for you to trust in yourself again."

"Like I mentioned, easier said than done. Let me grab my riding boots and hat, and I'll meet you at the barn." Erica disappeared inside again.

Adam smiled. Erica's determination to do well was a good sign, even if her reasons were all wrong. But then again...were they wrong? She wanted to do well in front of him, and he was doing things to help her. It's like they both had the right motives and simply had an interesting way to show it.

It hadn't gone unnoticed that the whole town seemed willing to keep the truth about Joy a secret for a little while, giving Adam the benefit of the doubt for his motives.

Everyone...except Ralph. Why he didn't reveal the truth was concerning. Unless it was altruistic in that it served his purpose to ride off into the sunset with a beautiful woman who would be completely dependent on him. Or the opportunity to make a lot of money, considering he was charging her double the going rate for the journey.

Chapter Seven

♥

It had taken Erica every ounce of courage to go back out on the porch, stop Adam from leaving, and admit her fears and inadequacy to him. His understanding and encouragement had gone a long way to keep her from turning tail and running back inside.

Now all she had to do was to see this stupidity through.

Not that a lesson was stupid considering she hadn't ridden since the summer she was sixteen. Asking Adam was the problem...but then he had been an excellent instructor all those years ago...in riding *and* kissing.

Her first kiss had been nothing short of spectacular...not that she ever told a soul. Not even her best friend, Laura. Extended riding lessons, away from the scrutiny of others, had given her the chance to get to know the real Adam. Handsome lad, charming to the core, yes...but there was more. His protective streak was a mile wide. He cared about people and animals, and his desire to connect with nature showed her the kind of person she admired. Someone unlike her father.

On many rides, he taught her about the birds and the bees...the completely innocent kind. Like how to identify cardinals, bluejays, eagles and so many other birds. And then there was the life cycle of the bee and how important they were to the environment. And then there was plant identification. From poison ivy to Maple trees to Rhododendrons, he'd shared his vast knowledge of the woods with her.

It wasn't until the last couple of days at camp that he had actually kissed her and promised he would see her again. And on the last day, he told her he loved her, and she had admitted to the same feelings.

Erica flung her sneakers into the corner of the room. It was the beginning and the end of something that could have been beautiful. Her parent's divorce was the end of Erica's childhood as she knew it. Even Laura had moved on with new friends.

And here she was now, ten years later, back in town and going riding with Adam, the man of her dreams. Ex-dreams, she clarified. *Talk about a full circle.*

Erica fired off a text to Ralph to cancel their trip. He would be upset at the loss of income, but then she was sure he would have no trouble finding consolation in the arms of the blonde woman.

It was more than a little relief she had felt when Adam showed up and offered to take her to Zeke's. Ralph was an odd sort, and not someone she trusted. He was an end to a means, and she had planned to stay on her guard during the trip. Now, it wasn't necessary. Adam, on the other hand, she totally trusted. Contrary to what she told him. Adam kept saying he had his reasons for never coming around after summer camp, and the problem was that Erica wanted to believe him.

It was the same reason she'd pined after him for years. Love had a way of doing that to someone. Lucky for her, she had no such problem now. They would be friends, which should be easy enough to remember, considering his love would always belong to Natalie.

Erica headed for the barn, her heart beating a little faster. Something she would do well to ignore. But the smell of fresh horse manure and hay assaulted her when she pulled open the door. Owning a horse wasn't easy, but it could be rewarding. If only she didn't have the bum foot and leg. She'd give anything to turn back the hands of time and get a do over. Move faster. Pay closer attention to what was happening at the base she was stationed at.

Erica didn't deserve Joy...or happiness. Molly had been the closest thing she had to a military best friend, and Sam was a comrade-in-arms. The two would never be home again to celebrate life and holidays with their families. Never be happy.

All the more reason to bring this fiasco of a gift horse to an end.

Adam looked up at her approach. "I've saddled Joy for you."

"Thanks. So, what's first?"

"Come meet her, for starters." Adam grinned.

Erica approached. "We've met. What's next?"

"A proper meeting. Joy, meet Erica."

Erica flinched when Adam took her hand as she tried to pull away. She looked into his steel-blue eyes and suddenly felt like she was sixteen again. With a shake of her head, she dispelled the image. "Okay," is all she could reply, finding it hard to concentrate.

Adam gently placed her hand on Joy's nose and helped her trace a smooth stroke down the bristly but yet soft white blaze. Joy raised her head and sniffed at Erica's hair, nudging her. The move made Erica laugh, but she quickly regrouped. "She's sweet and friendly."

"She is wonderful," he said, full of awe and wonder.

"How do you know?" Erica asked, suddenly on guard.

Adam seemed about to say something and then thought better of it. He shook his head and smiled. "I've spent the last fifteen minutes talking to Joy and telling her all about you." He chuckled.

"Hopefully good things," Erica quipped.

"Nothing but the best." Adam led her to the left side of the horse, allowing her to stroke Joy's flanks and back. She ran a hand through her mane. The mare was loving the attention, as she kept nudging Erica. It was as though the horse was trying to connect with her, which was ridiculous. There was no way Erica was going to believe in some silly legacy.

Besides, this whole endeavor was to give the horse away...not bond.

"Lead her out of the barn and let's get started," Adam said, placing the reins in her hand. And just like that, Joy followed. The horse was most likely eager for a ride on a beautiful day like today, so who could blame her?

They stopped, Adam moving next to Joy. He formed his hands into a makeshift stirrup to help Erica up.

If she put her left foot in his hands, all her weight would be on her right foot, but then she would need to push up with her left, something that would hurt, or worse, give out under the strain. "I don't think..."

"It's okay. Trust me on this. If you use me, like an extension of your left leg, it will all work out," he explained.

"But—"

"Just do it. And put your hand on my shoulder to help stay steady. It's okay to have help."

"Fine." Erica placed her hand on his shoulder to help brace for the pain of the move, but true to his word, none came. He was like a rock, his solidly built frame and muscles unmoving as he lifted her upward. Once in the saddle, she let out a deep sigh of relief. "Thank you. Now what?" she asked, trying to cover the awkwardness of the situation.

"Sit squarely, back upright. Use a small amount of leg pressure to get Joy moving forward. Feel the connection between your legs and her muscles. That's it. Relax. She can feel your every move. Trust her and she'll trust you. That's it," he said, smiling up at Erica.

Okay, so this seemed less daunting than she expected. In fact, it felt lovely to be up on a horse again. Erica looked around, enjoying the sights. She leaned forward and rubbed Joy's neck. "Thank you, girl." The mare nodded her head, as if in understanding.

Adam called out instructions, and Erica did everything he said. It was as natural as breathing. "I told you it was like riding a bike, and you would remember. It's time we go for a ride. A quick trial run. Just try to remember everything we've gone over, and trust Joy. Let yourself think and feel the connection and communicate with her." He was pulling off the kid gloves after only twenty minutes, which in itself gave Erica a boost of confidence. He believed in her, which is more than she did for herself.

The ride was refreshing. She stayed close to the house, and moseyed around the pasture, and just as Adam instructed, she gave into the connection with Joy. It was then that Erica realized something she hadn't thought of before. On a horse, her legs didn't matter. She could go places without pain. Be normal.

Maybe she was a fool to give away such a precious gift.

An image of riding off into the sunset was surreal...but then, so was the image of the man riding next to her.

Adam.

An unwelcome sense of Déjà vu hit. Erica turned the horse back toward the barn. "Let's go, Joy. That's not a path I can ever go again." *It was a good thing Adam couldn't read her mind.*

Chapter Eight

♥

Daylight came early in Alaska, but the radiant warmth was always far behind. Adam parked in front of the Carter's ranch house and slid out of the truck. He fully expected Erica to be ready and waiting on the porch, so it came as a surprise when she wasn't, though her belongings were neatly piled to the side. Raising his hand to knock, he moved back as the door pushed open to make room.

"Good morning," Erica said in a rush. "Sorry I wasn't out here. Getting ready took me longer than I expected. But then, I see you haven't unloaded the horses yet, so my timing is perfect."

Adam smiled, not surprised at her exuberance. "Good morning. I thought we'd do this in reverse, seeing as I live closer to the trailhead that we will be using. We can transport Joy to my place to save time."

Erica pushed her long brown hair back from her face, her cheeks prettily flushed in pink. "Oh. Makes sense. I could have ridden to your place if I'd known."

Adam shook his head. "That would add another thirty minutes and tire Joy out unnecessarily. This is fine and I don't mind. The other horses are saddled and waiting." He slung her backpack over his shoulder and picked up two other bags, leaving her just one small enough to go into her saddlebag. "Let's go," he said, stepping off the porch.

Adam headed for the truck, Erica falling in step next to him. He forced himself to walk slower. This trip would be hard enough for her with the injuries she had without Adam making anything worse. They put all her stuff in the back of the truck.

"Thanks. I've had trouble sleeping, but last night I slept amazingly well and would have hated to cut the time short."

"Ah, yes. The infamous beauty rest," he teased, shooting her a wink when she stopped to stare at him.

"In that case, I need hours and hours, not thirty minutes." Erica chuckled.

"Fishing for a compliment?" The banter reminded him of when they were at camp together.

"Hardly," she quipped, frowning at him.

It would be easy to do, as Erica had always been beautiful. Her bright eyes and fresh smile only accented what God had already given her. "I'd be more than happy to produce one."

"Save them for someone who cares," she said, shooting him a grin.

"Well, okay then. Guess that settles it. No compliments for the lady on the trail." Early teasing was a good sign the trip would start out on an even keel.

Adam pulled the truck closer to the barn. They headed inside, and he slid the lead over Joy's head and led her into the horse trailer, Erica following close behind as she brought out some of the other equipment necessary for a three-day trail ride.

After securing Joy, he stepped out. "I'll get the saddle and we'll be good to go."

"Thanks, Adam," she said, relief evident in her eyes. All she had to do was ask and he would have done it all, but he also knew Erica was full of pride and would have bristled at his assumption. Any help had to be initiated by her.

He mentally ran a checklist as she loaded the items in the back of the truck. Bridle. Reins. Blanket. Saddle bags. Rope.

She'd done good for someone who hadn't ridden a horse in ten years. He had always told her she was a natural and that good common horse sense went a long way.

Satisfied, he headed back into the barn for the saddle and tossed it into the truck. "Ready?"

Erica paused and looked up at him, a frown marring her lovely face. "Adam, do you think I can handle this?"

Adam schooled his expression to remain neutral. "You were always an excellent rider. You could cancel the trip and simply keep Joy. Might be nice for you to experience the awe and wonder of riding again. Not to mention she was a gift."

Erica shrugged. "I don't like charity. Too many other people need help, while I'll be just fine. Eventually, anyway."

"There are different kinds of healing...emotional and physical."

"I'm well aware of that, Dr. Landon. You, of all people, however, know how hard it is to handle a horse. I can't even get around without issue, much less trying to do physical labor. I'm not sure I'd be any good mucking stalls, carrying bags of feed or bales of hay. Can you imagine me trying to push a wheelbarrow with this bum leg? I'd wind up back in the hospital. And trust me, that's the last thing I want."

"There are ways around everything you mentioned. Hire someone to help you. You've also got your aunt and uncle. And me. Let people help you."

"I refuse to rely on anyone else. And what if something happens while I'm out riding? I'm in no position to manage any issues that might arise."

She had a valid point, but people couldn't stop living for fear of something going wrong. "And who's to say something would happen? And as to your refusal to let others help, that's something you need to work on. Life is never easy, but it's a whole lot better with family and friends to support you."

"I'm not looking for an easy life. I just want peace. Is that too much to ask? Enough talk. Let's go, cowboy."

"You got it, boss."

Erica moved to the passenger side of the truck, and Adam was right there for the assist. He knew better than to say a word, judging by the stiff way she held herself. After she was safely tucked inside, he closed the door and made his way around to the driver's side.

The ride back to his place was done in silence, proof he might have pushed a little too hard. So much for the earlier camaraderie. It would be a long three days if he didn't ease the tension between them.

Soon enough, they were back at his place. Adam led Joy from the trailer and handed the reins to Erica before saddling her. "Are you going to talk to me again? I'm not trying to make you mad. More like help you."

"Help me do what?" she asked finally.

"Figure out where you go from here. And how to deal with the emotional pain that keeps you withdrawn from life."

Erica frowned, a heavy sigh escaping her lips. "Last I heard that was Joy's reason for being here, not yours."

"Point taken." He tied Ginger's lead rope to the horn of his saddle, giving the extra horse plenty of room between them. "I won't say another word." *Maybe.* He moved to stand next to Joy and offered his hands as a stirrup, much the same way he had before.

Erica let out another deep breath. "You don't have to keep doing this."

Except they both knew he did. "No, you're probably right. But this way, we don't push your injured leg any harder than necessary, which will serve us both well in the end."

Erica's mouth tightened, her thin lips forming two straight lines. She might not want his help, but at least she wasn't saying no. "Fine. Let's go."

Adam rechecked Jasmine's saddle and stirrups and then, using the stirrup, slid into the saddle. He turned Jasmine toward the trail and clicked his heels against her flanks, leaving Erica to follow.

Jasmine was named after Natalie's favorite perfume, and it was times like this the memories of his fiancé flooded him the most. A time when he could look to the heavens in solitude and pray. Or just talk. He could almost smell the perfume lingering in the air. It had filled the house he'd bought her in town, the same house he sold not long after her death.

Natalie wanted the white house with a picket fence and to fill it with two children. The picture-perfect family. Something she didn't have growing up. Not with Maureen breathing down her back every step of the way after her father died.

Adam agreed to sell his home on the outskirts of town, but only after they got married. And after a year, Natalie hadn't even set a date, instead putting all of her time into organizing the Sidekick Squad Connection. Propriety wouldn't allow him to spend the night until after they were married.

He twisted around in the saddle to check on Erica. "You okay back there?"

"Sure thing. I'm just trying to remember what we went over yesterday."

Adam smiled. "Relax. It will all come back to you as naturally as it did when you were younger." The trail widened, and he moved to the side to allow Erica to draw near.

"Thanks. What's your horse's name?" she asked.

"Jasmine. She's my lead trail horse for the business."

"I love the white stripe down the nose. In a way, it's quite close to the blaze Joy is sporting, though Jasmine is a much darker brown. It's a striking combination with her dark mane."

"If you say so. I didn't buy her for her coloring." Adam chuckled.

They rode in silence for several minutes, Adam searching for a safe topic.

Erica pulled up close, riding even with him. "You know, you keep talking about wanting to help me, so why don't you help us settle up with the past? I know it's not our favorite subject, but can you tell me what happened? Did I do something wrong?" Erica asked, a flash of pain in her eyes.

Not exactly what he considered a safe topic. However, Erica's voice gave away her insecurity and almost caused him to tell her the truth. But he wouldn't be the one to drive a wedge between her and her father, especially since it was ancient history. "Absolutely not. You were sweet, full of life, and practically perfect. It was all about me, but some things are better left unsaid. Instead, why don't you tap into your memory and see what you can remember in identifying some trees, birds, and flowers?" They were talking again, and he wanted to connect with Erica, not push her away.

"Obvious change in subject accepted...but not forever. Consider yourself warned," Erica said, her unwavering stare letting him know she meant business.

"Warned."

They spent the next few hours searching the sky for birds and the trail for bushes and trees to identify. Adam loved the fresh pink glow on Erica's cheeks from the brisk cold and sun. All hints of sadness had vanished as she became one with Joy, whether or not she understood that. It only reinforced that he'd made the right decision not telling her the truth about Gilly...or his part in all this. Erica's well-being was far more important.

"Whoa," Adam gently instructed Jasmine as they neared Folly's Gulch. "This isn't good." He pointed to the rushing water. "Recent rains have really got the river moving faster than I expected. We can't cross here."

"Is there a better place? Will this slow us down?" Erica asked.

He nodded. "There's a place up the river that will take us about forty-five minutes to an hour to reach. It narrows there and it should be better. Unfortunately, that means forty-five minutes back in this direction after we cross. Not to mention it's almost time to stop for lunch and to rest the horses." This would put them way behind schedule, but it's not like they had a choice. Adam wouldn't risk the danger to the horses or themselves crossing the rushing river here.

"I see. Maybe once we get on the other side, we can make up time."

"Maybe. But we'll figure it out as we go. No turning back now unless you've reconsidered," he asked, hoping she'd agree to end the journey and keep Joy.

"Nope. Not a chance."

"All right then." It was worth a shot. The only part he hadn't told her was that based on timing, they might very well be sleeping on the trail tonight instead of in comfortable beds at his friend's place. Mack was expecting them, but he also knew the lay of the land and rigors of the trip. He wouldn't worry about his no-show guests unless they didn't show up in the morning. "Now that we're by the river, make sure you let me know if you see anything out of place, or of concern. We need to keep our eyes and ears open."

"For what?"

"Bear. Moose. Fox. Wolf. Cougar. You name it, they're out here. They hang out by the water for obvious reasons. Salmon."

"Oh, dear. Will we be safe?" Erica asked, not as confident.

"Of course, if I have anything to say about it. Just be vigilant. Four eyes are better than two." Adam chuckled. He turned Jasmine in the opposite direction and started up the trail that followed the river North. It was narrower, and Erica was once again forced to follow him. It wasn't ideal as he would rather keep an eye on her, but there wasn't any other choice, seeing as she didn't know which trails to follow.

An hour later, they arrived at the new crossing area. Far more satisfied with what he saw, he held up his hand to halt Erica's progress. "Let's cross here and then eat lunch. I packed some sandwiches so it will be a quick stop and the horses can get a drink."

"Sounds lovely, considering I'm starved. I can't remember being this hungry in a long time." Erica laughed, the sound rippling over Adam's skin like warm butter on toast.

"Trail riding is tough work, especially when your muscles aren't used to it. How are you holding out? And I need the truth please...no sugar coating the details. It's important I know if I'm going to keep you safe."

Erica bristled. "I'm fine," she ground out.

Tough as nails and unwilling to let down her guard for a second. It's not that he didn't notice the lines of tension on her face...he did. But he trusted her to tell him when enough was enough. It would be easier to keep a closer eye on her once they got back on the double trail.

Adam rode Jasmine through the water, slowly and giving her time to find her footing with each step. All three horses knew the routine. It was Erica that he was most concerned about. He turned to watch her cross, pleased when she held herself upright, but not tense. Joy would understand the message. Erica was giving the horse complete control to make the crossing and since Joy was the more experienced of the two, it was a good decision. "Nice work."

"It helps when you have a good horse. Joy is perfect. Not like the grumpy horse you used to make me ride." Erica's smile was firmly back in place.

Adam chuckled. "That grumpy horse was the only one I trusted you on when we went out on longer rides. You'd be grumpy too if you dealt with irritating kids all day."

"You always seem to bring her around and make her mind."

"Showed her who was boss is all," he teased.

"Showed her a carrot, or an apple is more like it," Erica retorted.

"You knew?"

"Of course. I thought it was sweet. It's one of the reasons I fell—"

"For me?" Adam finished for her. The idea gave him great pleasure, something he got little nowadays.

"Off my horse. Trying to see what you had in your hand," Erica said, grinning.

It was a quick recovery, but which was the truth? He much preferred his version.

"What's with all the salmon? I've never seen so many in one place," she asked.

"They move upriver to spawn. That's why there are so many animals hanging around...free and easy food."

"It was kind of cool. And Joy didn't seem to mind at all. I never got to do this sort of thing when I lived here as a kid. My parents weren't out-doorsy people, which perhaps explains why they couldn't cut it living in Alaska."

Adam helped Erica off her horse, setting her down on the ground gently, and giving her time to get used to being on her own two legs. "To be fair, it's not an easy life." He grabbed a blanket and spread it out on the rock, followed by the saddle bag loaded with a ready-made lunch. Sandwiches, nuts, water, and chocolate no-bake oatmeal cook-ies for dessert. High-protein foods with a little sweet indulgence.

Erica lowered herself onto the rock, her moves stiff and awkward.

Adam resisted the urge to help, knowing she would hate it. He dropped down next to her, grateful for the radiant warmth of the sun. Reaching into the pack, he handed her a sandwich.

She unwrapped it and took a bite, savoring the flavor. "*Hmmm*. My favorite."

Adam was pleased he had thought of it this morning, as anything to make Erica happy was okay with him. "I know. Somehow, I doubted you'd changed over the years."

"*Hmmphh*. I've changed a lot, but food, nothing beats PB & J. And I'm really glad it's not like a salmon salad or anything weird," she said, shooting him a grin before she took a sip of water to wash it down.

"Glad to know you're enjoying lunch. Unfortunately, I've got news you're not going to like." Might as well get the bad news out into the open. There was no way they could make up time. It would be too much on Erica and the horses.

"Oh, what's that?" she asked, her sandwich midair, her eyes wide open.

"The delay cost us just enough time that we can't push to make it to Mack's place by nightfall as planned. When the dark closes in, it will get freezing up here in the mountains and we need to be prepared."

"So, what do we do, mountain man?"

"We'll ride as far as we can and then stop for the night. I brought emergency provisions, so we'll be fine," he added to reassure her.

"You were always prepared for anything."

"I like to think I am, but sometimes life has a way of sneaking up on you." Like the night he lost Natalie. It was a night that changed his life forever.

Fortunately, someone had gifted him Sundancer's Joy, and it was with the mare's help he had finally made peace with that which he couldn't change. Instead, he'd turned all his energy into making Natalie's dreams come true. Which is why he had to get back to town on schedule, and this would set them back a full day. It would barely give them time to make it, but it was still doable.

The fundraiser was the final piece of the puzzle, and the money raised would help establish the program for years. Provided everything went according to plan. Which meant keeping Maureen out of the way and under control.

Something easier said than done.

Chapter Nine

♥

"Let's stop here for the night. I want to fix dinner and get hunkered down before it gets too dark. It will be cold, but nothing the sleeping bags can't handle," Adam said, sliding off his mare before he headed in Erica's direction to help her dismount.

Erica knew his intentions, as it was a regular pattern, but it didn't change her attitude one iota. She still stiffened slightly as he approached and held out his hands to form a stirrup assist. It's not that she didn't appreciate his concern and overly protective side, but it equally served as a reminder of her injury, leaving her feeling needy and less than self-sufficient. It was a hard adjustment after her military career.

"Sounds good." Truth be told, her leg and foot were throbbing unbearably. Adam's help might just be what she needed to keep from making a fool of herself. It was way past the time for her medication, but then it was like she could have called a halt to the trip just for that purpose. They were already behind schedule, and she had promised Adam they would be back in time for the fundraiser hosted at his home.

Placing one hand on his shoulder, she pushed out and away, putting her weight on the good leg. Adam was there, hands on her waist, ready and able to assist her to the ground. Effortlessly. He lingered, their gazes locked. Part of her wanted to reach up and caress his cheek, but the past stood between them like a brick wall. And she wasn't strong enough to knock it down.

Adam stepped back. "I'll get the fire started so you can warm up."

"That sounds lovely." The ride today had been amazing, and Joy was a big part of the experience. But being with Adam while they traveled through the wooded countryside didn't hurt either. Not having ridden in forever, she was sore, and it felt good to be walking on two legs again, even if one of them was in its own kind of pain.

Adam was busy gathering wood from close by, while she retrieved her medicine.

"You've got a couple of choices for tonight. I brought a tent in case something like this happened and we were forced to sleep outside. Would you prefer the privacy of a tent or to sleep under the starry Alaskan sky? You never know, we might even get lucky and see the Aurora Borealis if we can stay awake long enough," Adam said, using the sticks to build the base of the fire.

"Prepared as always," she teased. Erica thought it over and decided. "I wouldn't want to miss the opportunity, so if you really think I'll be warm enough, then sleeping under the stars sounds heavenly." It would be awkward, but nice.

Adam grinned. "These sleeping bags are good down to a negative fifty degrees. Along with the thermal blanket I brought, you'll be fine. The sleeping bags even come with a small built-in pillow. Everything is compact and lightweight for trail riding or backpacking in the mountains."

"Then it's decided. What can I do to help?" she offered.

"Warm up by the fire." Adam shot her a wink.

"Seriously. I'm not a total invalid, you know." The meds would kick in soon and she would be right as rain. *Unless it actually rained.* She viewed the sky for as far as the eyes could see. Not a cloud in sight. It would be a good night to watch the beautiful light show.

"Well, if you're up to it, you can lay out the ground cover and spread out the sleeping bags. Leave them fully zipped to avoid bugs and other critters and creatures we don't want sleeping with us tonight." Adam chuckled. "That will give me a minute to see if I catch us some fresh salmon from the river for dinner. Otherwise, it's PB&J again." He finished stacking another bundle of wood near the fire pit.

"Either is good, but the salmon would be amazing. When in Alaska...eat salmon."

"I'll make sure of it then. I would hate to disappoint the lady," he said, rolling up his sleeves to prepare for catching tonight's meal.

Adam unloaded the extra horse and piled up what was needed for tonight so she could arrange the bedding. Then he headed for the river with a net in hand.

Erica finished setting up the sleeping bags, deciding to lay them close to each other. The idea of being prim and proper held no appeal when compared to any late-night visitors. AKA animals that might want to eat her for dinner. Besides, she could zip up the bag tight around her face, just leaving her eyes, nose, and mouth exposed since it was a mummy sleeping bag.

Not that she needed protection from the likes of Adam. Honest as the day was long, sweet as apple pie, and the man was still in love with Natalie.

She moved close to the fire and warmed her hands. The flames had licked higher, their warmth welcome as the evening light dimmed.

Adam returned, carrying a huge salmon, surprising her. "Dinner," he said, holding it up for her inspection, a huge grin on his face.

"How did you manage that without a pole?"

"Caught it with my bare hands."

The glimmer of light in his eyes was from teasing or the firelight, and she was laying her bet on the first. "That's quite a fish story. More like you netted the poor thing."

"It's the truth. The net was just to carry the fish back up here." He sat it down on a rock and made his way over to Jasmine.

"I don't know. Sounds like a need to see it to believe it thing."

He pulled out a small camp grill, a pan, and some utensils, and picked up the fish. "Next time, you can watch, Miss Skeptical."

Now he was the one calling her names, and turnabout was fair play. But the one thing she didn't want to see was him preparing the fish. *Yuk.* "Hopefully, there isn't a next time. Otherwise, that would mean we won't be back for the fundraiser in time." She regretted the words the minute they were out of her mouth.

Adam's smile disappeared, the firm set of his jaw proof it was the wrong thing to say. "We'll get back...we have to. In the meantime, I hope you like blackened salmon?"

"I do. But who brings spices as part of their emergency supplies?"

"Trust me. I've been out here long enough to know how light the spices are when considered total weight hauled, but also how they can go a long way to changing someone's frame of mind.

It's like fine dining in the wilderness. All for a couple ounces in weight. It's a no brainer."

"I like the way you think." Erica laughed, unable to turn away as she watched him clean and filet the salmon, something he made look easy.

"I'll be right back. I just need to rinse the filets and get some water to rinse off the rock. That would be more of an animal attractant than either of us wants."

After he left, Erica warmed herself by the fire. When he returned, Adam spread out the current fire into a flatter area, reducing the flames. With the sticks, he formed two wide teepees, one on each side, to hold the grill plate. Talk about being efficient.

Such determination matched her own. Or once upon a time it did. Before the explosion.

She shook her head to dispel the negative thoughts, saying a prayer for God to grant her peace to accept the things she couldn't change. "You're handy to have around. Glad you became available."

Adam nodded. "I'm sure. Fresh fish and free...a clear winner in anyone's books."

"It's not just that, Adam. I'm glad it's you," she said, glancing up at him to see his reaction.

"Thanks. Does that mean you've forgiven me?" he asked, his voice filled with hope.

It was time to put the past to rest. "Yes. We were just kids. You keep telling me you had your reasons, and I trust you. Clearly not after you ditched me, but knowing you now, for sure."

"That means a lot to me, Erica. And for the record, I fully intended to come see you...before everything changed, that is. I'm just glad it all seems to have worked out best for everyone. You have a successful military career...had, I'm sorry. You did something important in your life and I think it's amazing. I am proud of what you've accomplished." Adam flipped the salmon carefully so as not to knock over his make-shift grill.

"The military was a good life. I traveled and saw parts of the world I may have never got to see otherwise. Made lots of friends along the way. I like to think I made a difference by serving our country. Until the accident. Now I don't know what to think anymore." She let out a heavy sigh. This wasn't her favorite subject, especially at night. She didn't want anything to set off a nightmare in front of Adam.

"You don't blame yourself for the accident, do you?"

Erica shrugged. "I don't know. I keep second guessing what I might have done differently."

Adam moved to stand close to her and take Erica's hand. "I think the purple heart you received tells the real story. Don't play the what-if scenario in your head. It will destroy you."

Erica flinched and pulled away. Blaming herself was exactly what she did. *All the time.* At least in the beginning, but now, she was keeping busy, and it didn't happen as often. "The medal doesn't tell the entire story or wash away the details I can't get out of my head. Let's change the subject. Some things are better left unsaid." She was using his own words against him.

"Okay." Adam removed the salmon from the fire and divided it between two plates, adding a scoop of canned baked beans. Piping hot on a cold evening. He put a kettle of water on the grill. The idea of hot coffee or tea held great appeal. She tasted the salmon, closed her eyes, and savored the fresh flavors bursting in her mouth. Grilled to perfection over a campfire. Who knew? Even the beans were delicious. Either that or she was starved. Or both. "I swear, this is the best meal I've ever had."

Adam laughed. "That's a stretch, but cold weather and campfires seemed to go hand in hand. Now you know why I consider spices a necessity."

"I do. Thanks again for agreeing to go with me."

"No problem. Can I ask you something?"

"Sure."

Adam sat down across from her, his gaze never leaving her face. "Why are you so determined to give Joy away? I mean, the real reason. Once upon a time, you loved riding and wanted a horse of your own. What changed?"

Erica didn't answer for a second, trying to put her reasoning into words. "The legacy. It's about hope and healing. Honestly, I think I'll be fine in time, and I don't need this kind of help. There must be someone more deserving of such a gift. And Joy is a special mare who deserves the right person to love her in return. She's such a special horse."

Adam nodded. "True. She is special. But so are you, and you deserve her. Don't sell yourself short. You're hard on yourself because of what happened, and you feel responsible. You hate the injury that makes you feel less of a person. I see the pain etched on your face sometimes, but yet you insist on not using a cane. I see the lines of tension deepen on your face and neck when I try to help you. And I see it when your smile disappears. It's time for you to let go of the memory and think of the future. Think of all the positives. You're back where you belong in Juneau. Your aunt and uncle love you. You have friends who care. And you're alive. So live. Find your joy again."

"Perhaps you should focus more on your own healing than on mine." She hadn't planned on snapping back at him, but he was coming too close to the real issue. She wasn't good enough to save her comrades, one of whom had been her best friend for the past three years. Ever changing tours of duty made it hard to keep lasting friends, and Molly had been awesome. Erica missed her friend's laugh. The memories of the fun they shared left her with a gut-wrenching emptiness.

Not good enough. Erica's new mantra rang loud and clear in her head every day since the bomb exploded.

"Perhaps. But since I care about you as a friend, I'm just trying to help. There's something inside of you that needs to be rediscovered. You once loved life and embraced every moment. It was your zest for life I fell for and that made you stand out, Erica. Don't let what happened change who you are forever."

He didn't understand. If she told him, maybe he would. Or not. "I grew up, that's all. It happens to everyone. Even you. Life changes people."

"I think it's more than that, but it's just my observation." Adam poured a cup of coffee and handed it to her.

"Thanks."

"You're welcome." Adam rebuilt the fire and pulled the sleeping pad and bags closer. "The temperature is going to drop fast. You might want to drink up and crawl into your sleeping bag to get it warmed."

All hints of the earlier discussion vanished. *Thankfully.* "Sounds good. Adam?"

"Yes," he answered, his voice husky and warm.

"Sweet dreams."

"You too."

Impossible if one of her nightmares hit, which she could only hope and pray wouldn't happen. Not with Adam close at hand and more than a little protective.

Chapter Ten

♥

Today's part of the trail ride was only the tail end of what couldn't be finished yesterday because of the issues at Folly Gulch. As a result, Adam took advantage of the opportunity for a slower morning schedule and got a small fire started. Nothing like fresh salmon mixed with MRE scrambled eggs. A luxury breakfast by some standards out in the wilderness.

Erica stirred, pushing back some of the sleeping bag that had covered all but the tip of her nose.

"Good morning, sleepyhead. Breakfast is almost ready."

"Good morning. I think." She yawned, struggling to get the sleeping bag unzipped further. "What time is it?"

She wasn't the slightest bit self-conscious about her appearance when she woke up, and his esteem of Erica rose another notch. "Six-fifteen. I reckon we can hit the trail and be at Mack's by nine. Then we can finish the journey to Zeke's and get back to Macks, where I'm hoping we can sleep in style and warmth before heading back the following morning." Adam grinned.

Erica covered her ears. "Too many details this early in the morning. I need coffee."

Adam poured her a mug full and placed it in Erica's outstretched hand as she finished sitting up. "Coming from a military woman. I would have expected you'd want nothing less."

"Retired military. As in...sleeping in is a luxury." She peered at the fire and inched closer.

"So is warmth in Alaska." Adam chuckled.

Erica nodded. "*Hmmm.* This hits the spot. What's for breakfast?"

"Salmon and eggs," he said, unable to hide his grin.

"Again?" she winced, scrunching up her nose. "For breakfast? Yuk."

"Fresh and free. It's a staple part of people's diet in the Alaskan backcountry, and good for any meal."

"I'll have to trust you on that one. It just doesn't..."

"Here. Try it." He handed her a fork and plate.

Erica stared at the food long and hard, then slowly loaded her fork. Halfway to her mouth, she stopped.

"Try it. You'll live," he teased.

"Haha." Erica took a bite, chewing ever so slowly. "It's not bad," she said, a begrudging tone in her voice, as she scooped up another bite. She took a sip of her coffee. "This is good and strong."

"Good deal. Only way I make it. I'll give you about twenty minutes to finish and get cleaned up down by the river. Then we need to be on our way." Hopefully, nothing else went wrong and they would be headed home tomorrow morning at the latest.

She nodded. "You sound like a drill sergeant."

"If we want to stay on schedule...someone's got to do the job." It would be tight, but making the fundraiser in time was still doable.

He moved off to feed and water the horses. After repacking the supplies, he was ready to go. Erica had followed his instructions to a tee, even cleaning her dishes. Her efficiency was expected, but still surprising to see in action. Natalie had been far more laid back, and as a result, everything happened later than planned. A trait he grew to love, remembering her soft laughter designed to make him forget his irritation with the delays.

"We're ready to ride." He offered his hands as a stirrup, a routine she'd finally come to accept without putting her on edge.

Erica hoisted herself up onto Joy's saddle. "You didn't wake me up last night, so I'm guessing the Aurora Borealis wasn't visible?"

"I was too tired to wake up and check. Not to mention, getting up in the middle of the night would make you feel the cold even more." He hadn't slept well, not by a long shot. It bothered him that Erica wasn't telling him what really happened in Afghanistan and why it bothered her so much. Healing came from letting go, something she didn't seem ready to do.

Not telling the whole story was the same thing he was doing regarding her father. Perhaps he should leave well enough alone. The last thing he wanted to do was drive a wedge between Erica and her parents. Divorce had a way of doing that on its own without his help, but then she was a lot older now. More prepared for the truth. It was something to consider.

"Tell me about the Sidekick Squad Connection program you're setting up. It sounds like such a great idea."

"It was Natalie's dream. She had a mentor when she was ten after her father passed away unexpectedly. The woman showed her a side of life that let her dream about the future. Moments of time to escape a not-so-good situation. Her mother can be quite tyrannical."

"So you say." Erica grinned.

"Trust me. Anyway, Natalie was determined to put together a program that would help lots of kids. Give them a chance to relax and enjoy life outside of their current situation. Single parents have it tough. This gives them a chance to breathe and let someone else shoulder the responsibility of parenting for a few hours. Like a refresher moment. Sometimes that's all it takes to fill the energy gas tank to get through another week of parenting responsibilities. Others are just unfortunate enough not to be able to afford extra things. The program allows kids to experience horseback riding, the zoo, the arts, entertainment, and cultural events. You name it." It was Natalie's dream, but also something Adam believed in wholeheartedly.

Erica nodded and smiled. "Wow. I had no idea it was so extensive. I'm so happy for the kids who will enjoy this special program. Kudos to you for sticking with it and fighting back against Natalie's mother. I still can't believe she doesn't see what an honor this is."

It was the same thing Adam thought, and everyone else, for that matter. *Except Maureen.* "She wants her daughter back. It's that simple. Unfortunately, that won't happen and she's living in the darkness. One day, I pray she will realize what you're doing and embrace the program. She has a lot to give and could be instrumental in its continued success. The woman is quite the powerhouse."

"Give her time. Healing comes to people differently. Parents expect to outlive their children, but it doesn't always happen that way. And it's a devastating heartbreak."

"I get that. I'm giving Maureen time to come to grips with the loss, but in the meantime, I'm fighting every cockamamie thing she does to stop me."

Erica nodded. "I'm sure you will raise what you need to make this program the best it can be. You always went all in when it came to something you wanted."

"True." Except for the time he wanted to ride off into the sunset with Erica, but needed to bide his time until she was old enough to know her own mind. And then...it was too late. Perhaps even then, God had already planned for him to meet and fall in love with Natalie. But then why take her away at such a young age? And before they had a chance to start their lives together?

And why was Erica suddenly back in his life?

Moments later, they exited the forest and were in a huge clearing. Talk about a picturesque view. One of Adam's favorites. Mack's small cabin and lake, surrounded by the woods and mountain views in the distance. Smoke poured from the cabin's chimney. His giant of a friend came out and stood on the porch waiting.

"Good to see you, Mack."

"Mighty good to see you, too. Thought you were going to be here last night. Almost went out looking for you, but figured you knew your way around and would be fine. Didn't hear any warning gunshots."

Adam slid off his horse. "You figured right." They shook hands, and then Mack pulled him into a bear hug. It was good to see him again. He moved to Erica's side to help her. "The river was too high at Folly's Gulch to cross. We had to do some backtracking, which slowed us down."

Mack shook his head. "Unfortunately, the same problem occurs up around Taku Bend. I talked to some locals yesterday who happened through here."

Fate was conspiring against him. "That's not good. I have no more time to lose. This is Erica Carter, by the way. We need to get her horse, Joy, to Zeke's place and then get back to Juneau without delay. Erica, meet Mack Trombley. He owns Mack's Trading Company. Without Mack, none of us would get our supplies out here in the wilderness to stock up on monthly."

"Quite an important man. Nice to meet you." They shook hands.

"Likewise. So why are you looking to get rid of Joy? Fine horse, if you ask me." Mack flashed him a quick questioning look before looking back at Erica.

"She was a gift. One I'm not ready to be responsible for."

Adam shook his head slightly, trying to send his friend a message to keep quiet. He'd answer all his questions later...privately.

"You don't like horses? Cause you rode in here like a natural and the two of you seem to fit together like you were meant to be." Mack was trying to understand but walking a dangerous fine line.

Erica shrugged. "Joy's like that. I mean, she's smart and experienced. Definitely knows how to make anyone feel like they can handle anything. She's been nothing short of amazing. Truth be told, I'll miss her, but like I said, I can't be responsible for a horse. There's too much going on in my life."

"*Hmmm*. Horses are a lot of responsibility for sure, but most people can fit in the time. What keeps you busy gadzook hours from sunup to sundown?" Mack was direct. Adam thought about stepping in to give Erica a respite, but opted to remain silent. More prudent would be to see if she let drop any information that would help him understand what she was facing.

Erica shuffled from side to side, hugging her midsection as a defense mechanism. "Actually, no. I mean, I just unexpectedly retired from the military, and I don't even know what I'm doing with my life at the moment."

"Even more reason to keep her, not give her away. And why Zeke?"

"Joy is one of the Sundancer's Legacy horses. I can only gift her to someone in need of hope and healing, and I don't have time to find that person. So, I decided to return her to her previous owner."

"What makes you think that's Zeke? Long way to go on a maybe," Mack said, looking between Erica and him.

Erica shrugged. "Trust me, I know. Folks in town seem to point me in his direction. If he's not the owner, then I guess I'll have to find someone. It just can't be me."

"Seems to me you got the horse for a reason. I've heard of the Legacy horses, and you must be a pretty special lady...in need of Joy. You know, there are lots of things you can do and still own a horse. Reckon if the horse was a gift...better not to look a gift horse in the mouth." Mack laughed.

"Maybe. That's what Adam keeps trying to tell me, but I still think this is for the best." Erica wasn't backing down from her resolve to return Joy.

"How's the river going toward Smuggler's Cove?"

Mack shook his head. "Not much better than Taku Bend."

Adam's heart sank. "If that's the case, we simply can't continue the ride. I'm sorry, Erica."

Hands on her hips, Erica glared at him. "But you promised."

"And you promised I'd be back in time for the fundraiser."

"But we have come this far already," she insisted.

"Hold up, you two. I've got a solution. I could fly you up to Windfall Lake," he said, pointing toward his seaplane. "Zeke's place isn't but an hour's hike from where I land. You could talk to Zeke, and then I can fly you back here. Just let me know if I need to run Joy up to him when the river slows down a bit," Mack offered.

"I'm not sure that's a viable option. Erica's dealing with an injury and it's not worth aggravating her leg or doing more damage," Adam said, nixing the deal right away to protect Erica.

The firm set of her jaw was a good indicator he'd struck a nerve. "Let me be the judge of what I can and can't do, please." Erica turned to fac Mack. "We accept. Thank you for such a kind offer. I've never been in a seaplane." Erica smiled at Mack.

"Anything to help the little lady." Mack chuckled. "Get ready for the ride of a lifetime, Erica. I'll even take the scenic route and show you a few glaciers in the process. I'm always in the air for business, so this will be a nice change."

"Yay. It's decided," Erica beamed.

Mack nodded. "Adam, if you'll meet me in the barn in about ten minutes, we can get the horses fed, watered, and turned out to the paddock." Code for...*you've got some explaining to do.*

Ten minutes later, Adam left Erica resting on the porch and headed for the barn, though he didn't have a clue what he would say. At least not to someone who knew and understood him as well as Mack did.

His friend glared at him the second the barn door closed. "What gives, Adam? You and I both know Zeke isn't Joy's current owner. What's with the farce? You know how I feel about shenanigans, and this one's a doozy." It wasn't often the two of them crossed words.

"It's not what you think. Or not exactly, anyway. Gilly gifted her the horse on my behalf, and I swear I knew nothing about it until after the fact. But it was a brilliant move if you ask me. The bottom line is that Erica has been through some pretty heavy stuff during her last military deployment. It's where she picked up the injury. I'm trying to help her get back on track. I said some things to Gilly, and he took it upon himself to deliver Joy. I had told him months ago to find someone in need of hope and healing. Once I discovered the truth of what happened, I wasn't about to undo what Gilly had set in motion. Erica needs Joy." Each time he repeated his well-meaning intentions, they seemed to lose luster. Surely, it wasn't wrong to help Erica the best way he knew how?

Mack shook his head. "That doesn't explain lying."

"I haven't lied. I didn't know a thing about it. I'm just not being forthcoming with what I do know. And for your information, I hate the ruse, but it's necessary."

"Explain," Mack pressed, not giving an inch.

"Trust me. If she knew the truth, Joy would end up right back in my barn, and then Erica doesn't get the help she needs. She's a proud woman. Very strong and independent. I just want her to have some time with Joy, giving them the opportunity to bond and change Erica's mind about keeping her. I know at some point I'll have to tell Erica the truth, but each day she spends more time with Joy, the more the two connect." Adam shoveled some hay into the feed bin, hoping to put an end to the conversation.

"Why? And what makes you an expert on what Erica needs? You just met the woman, far as I know."

Adam stopped and ran a hand through his hair. This is where it got tricky. "Not true. I met her when we were kids. I had just turned eighteen, and she was sixteen, when we met at camp." Adam could still picture her sweet smiling face as the two of them went on a riding lesson that inevitably got him back late for his next lesson. They could talk about anything and make it fascinating.

"Not exactly what I call kids. So, did you two date?"

"Nothing like that. I was a camp counselor, and she was a camper. I taught her to ride horses. She was a natural, and we connected. There were lots of rides...times we got to know each other, but dating was against the rules."

Mack raised an eyebrow, the questioning glint in his eyes more telling than words. "And..."

"And I kissed her. That's all, I swear. Well, except I told her I loved her," Adam added.

"And how is this all a problem now? What happened after camp?" Mack asked, still slightly baffled...and with good cause.

"I was so sure we were in love, and I promised to visit her after camp. We were going to date, but then, her father paid me a visit and demanded in no uncertain terms that I stay away from his daughter. I'm guessing she went home and told her parents about me. Long story short. I honored her father's wishes. It wasn't long after that her parents filed for divorce and moved away, or so I heard. I never saw Erica again. At least, not until she arrived back in town earlier this week."

"I still don't get why you feel so compelled to help her with Joy. Do you still have feelings for her?"

"I loved Erica. We were like two souls destined to be together. I understood her better than she understood herself at the time. And now, there's something missing inside of her. She seems lost in another world. One filled with pain and emotional trauma. I walked away from her before because her father demanded it, but this time, I won't walk away. I need to help her heal from whatever it is she's been through. Joy is my best bet to help her reconnect with life. To feel alive again."

Mack grinned. "What I'm hearing is that you're still in love with Erica. I sort of understand what you are dealing with, but I highly recommend you tell her about Joy...soon."

"I'm not in love with Erica now. I can't be. I love Natalie. But rest easy, my friend. I do plan to tell her before we get back to my place. I'll find the right time and explain why. Hopefully, she'll forgive me."

"Good. But Adam...Natalie's been gone a year and a half, bless her soul. Erica's here and now and you can find out if what you once felt was also real. You owe it to the both of you to find out."

"But Natalie..."

Mack clapped a hand on his back as they moved to the stalls, filling the water buckets. "Maybe God's giving you another chance at happiness, and you'd be a fool not to find out."

"It's not that easy," Adam said, his brain racing in a dozen different directions.

"Think on it," Mack said as he left the barn, leaving Adam alone with his thoughts.

"Am I doing the right thing, Joy?" he asked, rubbing the horse's head and scratching behind her ears.

Joy nodded, nudging his shoulder and then sniffing his pocket. "Sorry, no treats today, girl. But I'll let Mack know you deserve one."

Chapter Eleven

♥

Erica gripped the cushioned seat handles, her fingers turning splotchy white. She'd flown tons of times without issue, but this Cessna was a much smaller plane, and the floats replaced wheels. In the military, she had flown in the big boys, usually the C-130. She had even parachuted out of a C-17 during her parachute training. Of course, they had to pry her fingers off the door, but then somewhere about twenty-thousand feet, her fears let go of the deathly grip they had on her and she had enjoyed the ride the rest of the way down. Her landing, of course, was nothing less than perfect.

The windows were small, but more than enough to give her a dynamic view of everything around. The lake wasn't all that big, which meant little room for error. It wasn't like a runaway that went on forever, like at most airports. This was a case of get it right the first time. She placed the headset over her ears and listened as Mack explained some things to her and Adam. It would be like their own private guided tour. The whir of the props increased, and suddenly the plane was moving forward. Faster and faster, and without warning, they were climbing. It had been easy. No bouncing down a runaway. Just smooth and then lift off.

Erica let out the breath she'd been holding. So far, so good. They climbed out of the basin area and veered right. Below her in all its glory, the woods, the countryside, the river. And the majestic beauty of mountains were visible as far as the eye could see. The wall of snow-covered rock with scattered evergreens was serenely breathtaking. It was so peaceful. Like they were in their own world.

Minutes passed as Mack flew past the small glacier and then turned to the left. The ice was thick and rippled in one area, outcroppings of rock sometimes visible, but mostly hidden beneath the icy depths. Aquamarine pools of ice were scattered over the surface.

She would have liked to ask questions, but neither of the guys would hear her in the cockpit over the din of the twin engines. On the ride back, she fully intended to take Mack up on the offer to ride up front. Not that she would understand a single thing, with so many controls and gauges. For her, it was the view it would offer. Unparalleled beauty stretched out on the horizon.

They dropped in elevation as he flew over the river, the twists and turns breathtaking against the rugged wilderness. An eagle soared past in the distance. Erica was itching to take some pictures, but it was something she hadn't done in months. The accident had sucked the joy of capturing life in photos and cataloging her travels. The last pictures she had taken were of her friends who died in the barracks explosion. Molly laughing at something Sam had said as he made a face. The very idea of bringing them to life in a photograph somehow seemed wrong.

If only she could have discovered the deception of Sergeant Dahl sooner, she might have been able to save her two comrades. Extra minutes that might have saved everyone. Instead, she had lingered and talked with a few comrades on the way back from the mess hall. *Costly minutes she would never get back.*

Erica shuddered to think of the trust they all had in one another...a trust broken with such devastating impacts. She shook her head, trying to dispel the images and refocus on the beauty all around her. It wouldn't help to dwell in the past.

Mack's voice droned on as he recited the glacier's history as they crossed over them. Letting herself be immersed in the moment, she realized flying was as freeing as riding Sundancer's Joy. To a certain degree, both activities could be done with minimal use of her legs and feet. Although, flying would only apply if she were a passenger. But it was something to consider moving forward as she decided what to do with her life.

"We're coming up on Taku Glacier. It will be on your right. It's a good place to watch for a bear looking for an easy meal," Mack said. "It's reported that this glacier is almost five thousand feet thick and over 35 miles long. We'll be landing on Turner Lake, down there to the right a bit."

The lake below was even smaller than the one next to Mack's place. Erica watched in awe as they circled, coming in low, straightened and then landed on the water's surface. It was like parking a car at that point, as he swung around and pulled up alongside the dock. There were a couple of guys there to tie up the plane and greet them.

Mack opened the side door and let down the steps. He exited the plane and turned to help her, Adam right behind. She felt protected...and didn't mind. Talk about a novelty experience.

"Thanks, guys. That was awesome," she said, grinning like a bear who came up two-fisting salmon for his dinner.

"Glad you liked it. It's not often I get up here anymore, but it always amazes me."

"Which is exactly why neither of us will ever leave the area," Mack added. "Can't beat the rugged beauty of Alaska. You too go on. I've got a couple of things I need to take care of and then I'm going to hike up to one of my favorite spots. I'll meet back up with you here around six. It's three now, and that should give you plenty of time. We'll still have daylight to fly back."

"Will do. And thanks, Mack."

"Yes, thank you so much. I loved the experience," Erica added.

"Let's go," Adam said, taking her by the arm as they walked down the length of the dock. A move Erica didn't mind one bit. *Surprisingly.* "Mack was just telling me he made a few phone calls and has arranged for a Jeep to meet us here. They will give us a ride to Zeke's place and then back, so we've been saved from the long hike."

Erica paused, frowning at Adam. "Let me guess, you told him about my injuries?" This is exactly what she didn't want...to be treated special. As though she were an invalid incapable of life.

"We talked some, yes, but I didn't have to say anything in particular. You have a limp that sort of gives it away. You would do better to use the cane and give yourself a chance to heal faster."

"My decision," she said, unwilling to agree or discuss the matter.

"You're a hard-headed woman, Erica Carter. Always were." Adam shot her a wink.

"And you're a hard-headed guy. And stubborn."

"Touche. This way," he said, pointing to the Jeep parked off to the side. A man stood nearby, bundled up in his parka and fur hat.

"Hi there, I'm Adam Landon. You wouldn't, by any chance, be looking for us?"

"Yup. Mack caught me in the nick of time. Otherwise, I'd be headed to Anchorage, taking the wife and daughter shopping. Much prefer this, four-wheeling through the wilderness. Mack says you're headed to Zeke's?"

The man looked to be in his late twenties, his gruff beard in direct contrast to his jovial demeanor. Judging by the mud spattered all over the Jeep, the trails he rode weren't the dry, placid ones, more like crazy, fun-filled play in the mud trails.

Adam nodded. "Yes. We will want to be back on the plane no later than six, but I reckon it won't take us that long. Zeke's not expecting us. It would have been easier if he had a phone."

The man grinned. "Maybe. But then where's the fun in that? Zeke likes the quiet of the wilderness and figures in person communication keeps people closer. More personable. My name's Jimmy, by the way. I reckon Zeke will be happy to have company. Wasn't always that way after his wife died, but now, he's a changed man."

"Grief has a way of messing with your emotions and sometimes it's hard to dig your way out. I'm glad he's doing better."

Adam would know that life lesson the hard way...from experience. But then, so did she. "How far is it?" Erica asked, massaging her leg.

"Just about fifteen minutes. Way shorter than walking...and safer. The bears are active this time of year, so keep your eyes peeled. Maybe you'll be treated to seeing a mama bear and her cubs live and in action," Jimmy said, sliding into the driver's seat and leaving them to climb in on their own.

"That sounds lovely." Adam helped her into the Jeep, letting her sit up front. She wasn't going to argue the point, knowing the legroom would be better. The natural pull to have a camera at the ready for an exciting photo opportunity wasn't one she could tamp down this time. Unable to resist, she pulled her cell phone out of the bag she was carrying and slid it into her back pocket. *Just in case.*

And maybe on the flight back to Mack's, she would use this rare opportunity to take pictures of the glaciers. It's not like she'd be back this way and have another opportunity in the near future. *Focus on the positive.*

Jimmy chatted on and on as if they were old friends and the minutes flew by. All too soon, they were pulling up to a small cabin, having arrived at their destination. It was a huge disappointment they hadn't spotted a bear. But then, wildlife didn't dance to people's schedules.

An older man came out of the cabin off to the right of what appeared to be an old rustic, small single-story lodge. Several buildings were all grouped together. As they got out of the Jeep, the man moved forward to greet them. Dressed in an oversized parka, his gruff beard and thick gray hair practically covered his face. He sort of reminded Erica of Santa, but without the red suit.

"Zeke Haskins," he said, offering his hand to her first, and then Adam.

Erica took charge, since she was the reason they were here. "Hi, Mr. Haskins. I'm Erica Carter and this is Adam Landon."

"I know Adam. Good to see you again. It's been years. You're a long way from civilization, young lady. What brings you out here...with Adam, no less?"

"Good to see you too, Zeke." The two men shook hands.

"Well, Mr. Haskins—"

"Zeke. No one calls me Mr. Too formal for my liking."

Erica nodded. "Well, okay then, Zeke. I know this is going to sound far-fetched...or maybe not. Oh dear, I'm trying to figure out how to go about this."

The old man pushed his wire-rimmed glasses up on his nose, his gaze never leaving her face. "Shoot straight. Only way I play."

The moment of truth was upon her, except Erica wasn't feeling the overwhelming sense of relief she expected to feel. "This is about a horse. Sundancer's Joy. The mare was recently gifted to me and folks in town seem to think you owned her before I got her."

Zeke nodded.

Her breath caught in her throat. She had found Joy's owner.

"Except it was a long time ago. She hasn't belonged to me for some time now. What seems to be the problem?" Zeke glanced at Adam, a questioning look on his face.

Erica struggled to keep her racing pulse under control. If Zeke wasn't the one who gave her Joy, then this had been a fool's mission. "I can't keep the horse. I'm looking to return her to the rightful owner." Even as she said the words, she wasn't sure they were true anymore.

Adam wandered away, possibly to give her a chance to explain the situation to Zeke.

"I thought you said the horse was a gift. Not very friendly if you don't accept gifts. Not neighborly, if you ask me. Someone must think pretty highly of you to gift you a horse. Especially given that Joy is a Sundancer's Legacy horse."

"I'm just not in a position to keep a horse. There is so much going on in my life right now and I know nothing about what my future entails. Who did you give Joy to?"

Zeke looked away as though interested in something going on in the distance. "Sorry, that's always confidential information. I gave the mare away over eighteen months ago to someone who needed a healthy dose of hope and healing. I reckon you ought to embrace the gift, young lady. After I lost my wife and son, I didn't think I'd ever find joy in my life. That's when someone gifted Joy to me. The mare brought me back from the land of the dead and showed me reasons to embrace life. If I hadn't of done that, I wouldn't have discovered my son had a daughter of his own. My granddaughter. The light of my life."

Erica brushed away the tears that slid down her cheeks. "What a beautiful story. I'm sorry for your loss but so happy you found something to be joyful about. I just don't think—"

"If someone gave you Joy, they must feel you need some extra help. Nothing wrong with someone caring about you, is there?"

Erica paled. "When you put it that way, I feel bad for trying to return her."

"Or maybe the real problem is that you haven't admitted to yourself or anyone else that you need help to get through whatever it is you're dealing with?"

Talk about a punch to the gut. She didn't come here to get psychoanalyzed by a virtual stranger. "I—"

"Erica, trust me on this. Think long and hard before you make a decision you might regret," Zeke said, the old man clearly reading her mind.

Lucky for her, she didn't have to decide now. "Well, it would seem the decision is out of my hands since I can't find the owner."

"Blessing in disguise." The old man shot her a wink, his amiable smile back in place.

Erica breathed a sigh of relief. The subject was one she tried to avoid. "So, what do you do here? Seems sort of deserted."

"Four months out of the year, this place is hopping with tourists. The rest, I live peacefully with Mother Nature and take care of the place. And of course, spend as much time with my granddaughter as I can teaching her everything I know about the area, the history, and the culture. There's so much to Alaska and it truly can't be absorbed in a week's vacation." Zeke spoke with a reverence in his voice that proclaimed his love and passion for the area.

"I agree with you about Alaska and can't wait to learn more. When I was a kid, there wasn't much time for exploration. Except when I went to summer camp, and then that was quite limited.

But even that ended when my parents divorced and moved back to the mainland."

"Well, it's good you're back. I hope you and Adam will stay for supper. I've got some fresh salmon and I'm sure my cousin wouldn't mind a free meal after he finishes hosing down the Jeep. There's plenty of time to get back for the flight to Mack's place before nightfall sets in."

Erica wanted to say yes, but doubted there was time. "I would love to, but we're supposed to meet Mack back at Turner Lake by six."

"I can serve dinner a little earlier than usual if that helps. Don't get much company out here this time of year. Besides, we're bonded by Sundancer's Legacy now. Not many can claim that honor."

Erica smiled, genuinely relaxing for the first time since she arrived. "You've got me on that point. I wish we could have brought Joy here so that you could have been reunited, but Adam's got a hard deadline to be back in Juneau for the fundraiser. The river hasn't been cooperative when it comes to safe crossing points, so you'll have to ask him."

Zeke nodded. "I would love to see Sundancer's Joy. Perhaps some other time you'll bring her out this way."

"Of course. A friend of Joy's is a friend of mine," Erica said, realizing it was the truth.

"See that you remember that," Zeke said before walking away, leaving her to wonder what he meant by the comment.

The two men were in deep conversation, and Erica opted to explore the area. It was so beautiful, the green grass, the glaciers and mountains, the lake. Blueberry bushes grew wild, and the trees soared above her head.

Truly peaceful.

Erica hoped Adam agreed to stay, as she wasn't ready to leave this magical place. Not by a long shot.

Chapter Twelve

♥

Adam had never looked for his benefactor after Joy was delivered to the Wilderness Camp Lodge, but had always suspected Zeke. The gossip mill in Juneau extended far and wide, and Zeke's name had long since been linked with a legacy horse. And now he was sure of it. Not that it changed anything. He would be forever grateful to Zeke for helping him move past the pain enough to put his heart and soul into the Sidekick Squad Connection.

He was grateful Zeke hadn't outed him. All Adam wanted was for Erica to fall in love with Joy long enough to decide to keep the mare. After that, it was up to Joy to live up to the legacy. Lost in his own thoughts, he hadn't heard anyone approach until Zeke was standing next to him. The old man wasn't smiling, and Adam knew why.

"I'm surprised you came all the way here looking for the previous owner of Joy," Zeke said, his voice void of expression. It was the questioning look in his weathered, steel-gray eyes that spoke volumes. *Judgment for sure.*

"It's a long story," Adam said, tired of defending his choice to help Erica. Or the way he helped her, that is. He looked back at the lodge, making sure Erica wasn't within earshot.

Zeke's gaze was steadfast. "Try me, because we both know you're the owner she's looking for. You're playing the girl for a fool, and it won't end well. She's a smart lady and it won't be long before she puts it all together. Someone will tell her...accidentally or otherwise."

Adam shook his head. "Trust me, I agree with everything you're saying. The problem is, if she finds out I'm the benefactor, she'll return the horse. End of story. Joy can't work her Legacy healing if she's back in my barn."

"But she's—"

"Erica is lost in a dark world after returning from Afghanistan. All I know so far is that she was severely injured in an incident and refuses to talk about it. I want to help. No...I *need* to help her." Adam explained the whole story, much the same way he had to Gilly and Mack.

When Adam finished, he was surprised to see Zeke grinning like an old fool.

"So, you're in love with her?" the old man said, his matter-of-fact unsettling.

Except Zeke was wrong. "No. Why does everyone keep saying that?"

"Because it's written on your face when you look at Erica. It's in your voice when you say her name. Just because you don't want to admit something doesn't mean it's not true."

Adam shook his head. "There's no place in my life for love. I was in love with Natalie, and it didn't end well. But then clearly, you know that," he added, remembering Zeke as his own benefactor.

"What do you mean, it didn't end well? Were you happy with Natalie?" Zeke asked.

What kind of question was that? "I was until the day she died," Adam said, his voice void of emotion. It was better not to go down memory lane.

"None of us know when it's our time. Only God does. Consider yourself blessed to have known and had the love of such a sweet woman. Her death doesn't take away from the happiness you shared when she was alive...it only makes it all that much more important. Priceless memories. Would you have wanted to miss the dance to avoid the pain?"

Adam pulled back, the question hitting home. "Well, no. But the story ended."

"Then start a new story. You're young. Natalie would have wanted you to be happy, the same way if the situation were reversed. Am I right?" Zeke pressed.

"I reckon." *It was true.* Adam would have wanted Natalie to go on living, but it was a hard truth to hold on to because the situation wasn't reversed. "Joy gave me the healing I needed to come out of hiding and face the world. I could push forward and finish what Natalie had started. I always thought her mother would do it, but I was wrong. For me, everything is about making Natalie's dream come true and has been for the past year. And I have you, apparently, to thank for the uplifting shove. Joy is amazing. I can't thank you enough for your gift."

Zeke nodded. "That's what I heard. But let me ask you this...what happens when the program is up and running? What's next for you?"

It was the same question Adam had asked himself a hundred times. "I don't honestly know. Focus on the guide business, I reckon."

"What about love? Where does it factor into your future? God delights in love for a reason."

For the past year, Adam had considered himself healed and living life once again. Joy had been such a blessing. His focus was on work and the program and there hadn't been time for anything else...especially not a relationship. "I've never considered it. Finding someone to love twice would be a miracle, and I'm not sure I'm up to it anyway."

"The world is full of miracles...just ask me about my granddaughter." Zeke said, his beaming smile full of wonder.

"Well, the miracle I'm praying for is Erica's healing. I met her a long time ago when we met at summer camp. I also know that whatever happened in Afghanistan left her broken inside, and I would give anything to see her happy again. Even at the expense of our friendship."

Zeke clapped him on the shoulder and nodded. "I rest my case."

"What do you mean?"

"You love Erica...even if you don't recognize it yet. But take it from an old man who knows...what you're doing might be a selfless act of love...but it's also foolhardy. Do some soul searching and figure out what's important...before it's too late. There's more at stake here than friendship. From the outside looking in, I can tell right here and now she cares about you too. Make sure you don't overlook the importance of her feelings."

This was something Adam hadn't considered. Spending time with Erica was enjoyable. More than enjoyable, though he was loath to admit it. What if Zeke was right? Would it change anything for their future? Or had Adam already burned any bridge with his omission of the truth? "I will give it some thought. Thank you."

"Why don't the two of you stay for an early dinner? I know you have to be back on the plane by six. Erica's game but says it's up to you. It'll give you both a chance to unwind before the return trip to town. Perhaps an enjoyable walk and a chance to talk." Zeke wasn't giving an inch, but this wasn't the time or place. If he told her, it would be on the return trip to Juneau. A time when she couldn't walk away from Joy...or Adam.

He nodded. "Sounds perfect. Thanks Zeke. For this...and for Joy. She was a true blessing."

"You're welcome. Let's hope one day Erica feels the same way." The old man chuckled before he turned away and headed back to the house.

Zeke was right about everything. It was only the letting go part that kept Adam in check. Somehow, it didn't feel right to move on. At least not yet.

He loved Natalie, but what if he had always loved Erica?

Adam found Erica rocking in a chair on the porch, looking relaxed and at peace with her surroundings. She smiled at his approach. Soft and sweet, a reminder of days gone by.

"What's the verdict? Are we staying for dinner?"

Adam nodded. "It would seem so. Once Zeke said you wanted to, I was all in. Anything for you," he said, sitting down beside her.

"That's not the way the story went a few days ago," she teased.

"Things change. I mean, I'm glad we've had this time together."

"Even if it was a fool's mission?"

"Hardly that. I mean, you're already smiling more. I believe that Joy and the fresh air have done you good."

"Maybe. Do you think Joy is okay? I mean, what if she's missing her owner?" Erica bit at her lower lip and frowned.

"Except that would be you, and you're still going to see her tonight. You can even take her an apple treat and tuck her in." Adam chuckled.

"It certainly looks that way, but you know what I meant. Do you think I'll be able to take care of her? Honestly. It's strange, but I feel as though she speaks to me. Encourages me to be brave. When I ride her, there's a sense of purpose. It's as though a unique bond falls into place and we become one...horse and rider...together against whatever comes our way. Does that make any sense...or do I sound silly?"

Adam shook his head. "Of course it's not silly, and it makes total sense to me. When you two are together, it's like poetry in motion."

Erica rolled her eyes. "Now I know you're full of baloney. I'm not that good of a rider."

"You're a fast learner. Always have been. Trusting each other is half the battle, and with Joy it seems to come easy. You just needed time to figure that out."

"Thanks. Maybe I should have accepted Joy in the first place...graciously. I do love her, and when I ride, I feel at peace. It's like she's my legs and I can do anything. Even fly. She makes me forget." Erica glimpsed down at her injured leg and foot, a reminder the injuries were real.

"That's amazing. Talk about progress. And it would seem the legacy is living up to its name."

Erica nodded. "So it would seem."

Perhaps now was a good time to tell her the truth. He hated to spoil the moment, but it had to be done eventually. "Erica, there's something I need—"

"Hey, you two. Dinner will be in about twenty minutes. There's a beautiful short trail alongside the glacier and then it cuts back through the woods. Can't miss the markers. Would be a beautiful evening for a walk and one you shouldn't miss. It's one of the guest's favorite activities when they visit," Zeke said.

"Sounds lovely. You game?" Erica asked, grinning.

So much for the discussion, but then, perhaps it was for the best. He didn't want to spoil the outing, especially not when she seemed so relaxed. Happy, even if only for the moment. "Of course. Shall we?" he said, offering her his arm to hold on to.

"The trail head starts there," Zeke said, pointing to a sign down by the lake. "I've got walking sticks if either of you wants one."

Erica hesitated, pondering the offer. "I'll take one."

Perhaps a walking stick didn't scream injury, but whatever had her saying yes, Adam was inwardly excited. Talk about progress.

Zeke pulled one from the urn by the front door and handed it to Erica. "Have fun's quite romantic, I'm told."

"Do you think he's playing matchmaker?" Erica asked, laughing up at Adam.

There was no thinking about it. Zeke was in full-blown matchmaker speed. "Seems like a safe bet, but then, I reckon it's all about making the tourists happy."

"*Hmmm.* Maybe," she nodded, her smile slipping slightly. "It's so peaceful here."

"That it is." He walked slowly, holding her free hand, letting her set the pace.

He stopped at the first scenic overlook, a small section of the Taku glacier up close and personal. They could see the cracks and crevices and hear the calving sounds as chunks of ice broke off and dropped into the lake.

"You started to say something on the porch...what was it?" Erica asked, glancing up at the birds overhead.

This wasn't the right time. "It was nothing."

"Okay, then. Any chance you'll tell me about what happened after camp? I would really like to know, Adam."

He started to pull away, but she held his hand, not letting go. "Erica…"

"Please." It was the soft lilt of pleading in her voice that caught and held his attention. The woman earned a purple heart for bravery in the worst of times.

"Okay. You win. You won't like it, but you deserve to know the truth. Your father warned me off, as in demanded I stay away from you." Adam watched her closely, hoping this wouldn't spoil the moment.

"My father?" she asked, her expression one of disbelief.

"He came to see me the day after camp ended. I can only guess you said something to your parents about us. And after the one-sided conversation, it was clear I only had two choices. His way or he'd make my life miserable since I was eighteen and going off to college, and therefore, too old for his sixteen-year-old daughter."

"No way. I mean, yes, I came home telling them about you. I was in love and wanted to share my happiness. I'm so sorry. This is not at all what I expected. All these years, and it was my father's doing? You should have told me." She dropped his hand and pressed a fingertip to one temple, massaging it with slow circles.

So much for the peaceful moment. "And risk him following through with calling in the law? Not a chance. I figured I would run into you and have the chance at some point, but then the next thing I knew, you moved away. It was as though we were never meant to be, and I believed God had different plans for us. I'm so sorry."

"There's nothing you need to apologize for. It's me. All these years, I was so angry with you. Hurt. Broken-hearted, truth be told. The fact it all happened at the same time I found out my parents were getting a divorce made it worse. Then we moved. I was so mad at you for deserting me, but perhaps it was easier to blame you for everything. As though hating you was like having a great big punching bag for a teenager whose parents were getting divorced. I'm sorry. I should have believed in you. Trusted my heart that something wasn't right, and as you just mentioned...trusted God."

Adam reached for her hand and drew her close. "How could you? Everything was new between us, Erica. But I swear, it was real. Never doubt that."

Erica nodded, her eyes glistening with unshed tears. "Thank you for telling me, Adam. Do you ever wonder what would have happened if we started dating?"

"I did...all the time. Until I met Natalie. She helped me forget you and move on in the real world," he said, his voice soft and low, knowing it was the truth. *Or had been.* But what if Zeke was right, and that with Erica back in his life, they might have another chance at love and happiness?

"Natalie must have been a very special woman to win your heart."

Adam nodded. "She was. Kindness personified in and out to save the world. Natalie was a most amazing woman who lived life to the fullest, honoring God every day in her actions and words by helping others."

Erica reached up to cup his cheek, the gesture almost his undoing. A tenderness he hadn't felt in a very long time stole over his heart.

"No wonder you fell in love with her. You always had a soft spot for people looking to change life for the better," she said.

Adam's hand closed over hers. "Exactly. Like you, only your way was a lot more direct. Serving in the military is not for the faint of heart, and it's something to be proud of." He kissed the back of her hand ever so softly.

Erica blushed, her cheeks and throat turning various shades of splotchy pink. "Thank you. I just wish it didn't end the way it did," she added.

They started to walk again. "You can't change the past, only learn to live with the positives that you can take away from that time." Zeke's words echoed in his head, clearly having left a lasting impression on Adam.

Erica nodded. "The same applies to you."

"True enough," Adam said, stopping again to take in the glacier's beauty, the shimmering water, and the beautiful woman standing next to him.

"Erica..."

"Adam..." they said in unison.

"You first," he said.

Erica nodded. "Can we be friends? I mean, for real? It would mean a lot to me."

Adam felt as though a weight had been lifted from his chest. "I feel the same. We can't turn back the hands of time, but we can push a restart button." All the more reason to tell her about Joy.

"I'd like that," she said, a beautiful smile lighting her face.

"Good." He tried to get up the nerve to broach the subject.

The dinner bell clanged on the front porch. "We should head back. Sounds like our twenty minutes are up." *A saved by the bell moment*. Any conversation to clear the air would have to wait.

They moved along the path, setting a quicker pace but still not breaking any records as Erica safely maneuvered the twists and turns and roots of nearby trees. As they cornered the barn, Adam pulled back, grabbing Erica's arm. A bear was on the grill where Zeke had been cooking the salmon.

"*Shhh*," he said, pointing out the bear. Seeing a wild bear up this close was naturally unnerving, but he'd had enough run-ins with them to know the bear's first concern was the salmon, especially as there was no bear cub in sight.

Erica stepped partially behind him. "Oh, my. She's beautiful. Look at the way the sun is glinting off her brown fur, making it a reddish brown. "

Adam laughed. "She's actually called a cinnamon bear. We should move to safety before the bear finishes its snack. I'm guessing that's our dinner she's polishing off."

"Wait." Erica looked torn between leaving and her fascination with the bear, having grown more confident and moving to stand beside Adam.

"What is it?" he asked.

"I...I want to take a picture."

"Sure thing. Make it quick though."

Erica pulled out her phone and snapped a picture. Then a couple more. The hesitation and frown on her face didn't match up.

"Why don't you like taking pictures? Once upon a time, it was another one of your passions. I remember you taking hundreds of photos."

Erica shoved the phone back in her pocket. "We should get going."

"I agree. Tell me what's going on? You wanted to get pictures, but then it seemed as though you hated taking them. I'm confused." Adam led her around the barn. It was a longer walk to the house, but it was safer.

"I stopped after the accident. I don't want to bring photos to life anymore. At least not until just now. The bear was amazing, and I couldn't resist. It was the power of the moment."

"He's amazing for as long as he doesn't decide to eat us," Adam teased. "As for taking pictures, it's a part of who you are. Like breathing. Don't forget that."

"Where are we going?"

She ignored his comment...or didn't care to discuss it. Either way, it was the truth and hopefully she'd figure it out for herself. "The path here will take us back to the lodge a different way. Zeke will worry when he doesn't see us, but we'll be back momentarily and put his mind to ease."

Up on the porch, he pulled open the door and let Erica pass. Inside, they discovered Zeke intent on watching the bear from the window.

"Does this mean our dinner is history?" Adam asked.

"Glad you two are back and okay. Saw you coming, but quickly realized you had the situation under control. And no, dinner is fine and I'm keeping it warm in the kitchen. The bear is licking all the salmon juices in the sand below where the cooling grate was. It's like a lollipop to a bear, and Tesla here can't get enough. Comes in about five minutes after I finish cooking. Got a keen sense of smell, that bear."

"Tesla?"

Zeke grinned. "That's what I named her. She's fast and efficient. And will be gone in minutes after the recharge."

Adam and Erica laughed, grinning at the sight of the bear as it lumbered down the steps of the grill landing and back into the woods.

An experience to remember.

But it was the woman beside Adam who was the best part of the memory.

Chapter Thirteen

♥

The flight back was as awe-inspiring as the first time around. With one big differ-ence...Erica didn't hold back capturing photos of the breathtaking scene below. It was as though the grandiose mountains and glaciers called to her, painting a bigger picture that soothed her weary mind.

They had barely arrived back at Macks before it grew dark outside, and she'd headed straight for the barn. Stopping only to grab a carrot, Erica had been reunited with Joy. The mare whinnied and nudged her, probably as much in a demand for the treat as the fact her new friend had returned. Erica rubbed the horse's neck and nose, scratching all her favorite places. After speaking to Joy for a few minutes and reassuring her they would get plenty of exercise tomorrow, Erica had headed for the house, eager for a good night's rest.

The warmth of the cabin was welcome, as well as the twin bed in the bedroom Mack had set up for her. Down comforters had blanketed Erica as she snuggled in for the night and she'd fallen asleep almost instantly.

This morning was a different story. Dragging back the covers wasn't easy, but Adam had already knocked at her door twice, making sure she was awake. He was eager to get on the trail, hoping to make up for some lost time. If she thought Joy could lead her back safely on their own, Erica would consider the feat just for the chance at a few more hours of sleep.

Throwing back the comforter, her feet hit the cold floor. She quickly dressed in layers, a trick Adam had mentioned. She ambled out of the bedroom, only to discover the guys had finished their pancake breakfast, and only her plate and a big stack of pancakes next to it waited for her. The aroma of coffee brought her fully alert as she went in search of the coffee maker.

She looked over at Adam as he entered the kitchen. "Good morning. Sorry I'm running behind. I could skip breakfast if it will help speed things up.”

"Morning. And absolutely not. You need your strength for the ride. Extra calories to counter the cold and exertion.”

Mr. Wilderness Guide reciting rule number six. Or was that seven? Erica lost count. “Lucky for me, Joy will do most of the work.”

Adam shook his head as he topped off his coffee. “You’re a team. I’ve already fed and watered the horses. They’re saddled and ready to go.”

"Aren’t you Mr. Efficient? Where’s Mack?”

"A moose came through last night and left some poop droppings. Made a mess all over the front yard. Mack wanted it cleaned up before anyone accidentally stepped into one of the piles and then tracked it into the house. Mack’s one of those guys who puts cleanliness as a top priority on his list. Cleanest mountain man you’ll ever meet, I’m sure.” Adam grinned.

"Mack’s a smart guy. Kind and helpful, as well. Quite the catch for someone.” She laughed, instantly embarrassed by her words as the man himself joined them in the kitchen.

"I'd like to think I am. Old age and wisdom go hand in hand. I like this woman, Adam. She's a keeper." He shot her a wink, and his ear-to-ear grin was more contagious than the flu.

Adam frowned at his friend. "Except she's not mine to keep Mack, and you know it."

Talk about a killjoy. "If you two are done discussing me as if I'm not here, I'd like to eat my breakfast in peace."

Adam headed for the door. "Meet me out front in fifteen minutes and be ready to ride."

"Yes, sir," Erica said, grinning at his backside as he left the room. "Is he always this pleasant in the morning?"

Mack chuckled. "He's fairly low key. I just know how to rile him up."

"Well, thanks. I'll be the lucky recipient of his good mood all morning."

"Sorry. I simply couldn't pass up the opportunity. We've been friends a long time, and we go back and forth hassling each other. It's not always me, mind you."

Erica dug into the pancakes. "*Hmmm.* These are delicious. You're forgiven."

"Why, thank you. It pays to know how to cook when you're living on your own," Mack said, without so much as a hint that his single status bothered him. Almost as though he was resigned to the fact.

"So, no special someone out here with you?"

Mack shook his head. "*Nah*. Reckon no woman will have me. They don't enjoy living remotely in the wilderness, and I don't enjoy living in town. Too many people, if you ask me."

Adam, too, had been like Mack. At least he had been until he'd fallen in love and moved to the outskirts of town. "One of these days, the right woman will discover all your talents and scoop you up."

"You applying for the job?" Mack grinned.

"Touche, but I think not." It wasn't just the age difference, there was also the little matter of Adam. Spending time with him wasn't at all what she expected. *It was better.*

"Adam and me, we're like two peas in a pod. We like our remote life. Though he tried going the town route for Natalie. Not sure he would have lasted, but love had him willing to try."

It was the same thing Erica had figured out. "Natalie was a lucky woman."

"And Adam was a lucky guy. He was a happy man until he wasn't. I'm glad to see he's come out of his shell. For a while, it was bleak. Holed himself up at the Wilderness Camp for almost six months before he jumped headlong into the Sidekick Squad Connection. He's almost himself, but not quite, if you know what I mean."

"I do." Erica was well-versed in her own version of falling short. Since coming to Juneau, however, she seemed to be managing small strides toward regaining her life. "The program means a lot to him. He told me it was Natalie's dream. Once it's up and running, I wonder what he'll do next?"

Mack stroked the gray whiskered stubble on his chin. "Probably run back to his cabin in the woods and go back to being a full-time guide. Unless someone gives him a reason to want more from life, that is."

"Someone?" she asked, regretting the question as soon as it was out of her mouth, knowing where Mack was headed with the conversation.

"I see the way you two look at each other."

"You've got it all wrong. Trust me. We had our chance a long time ago, and it didn't work out," Erica explained. She ate her last bite of pancake, and stood, moving to the sink to rinse her plate and hoping to avoid any further conversation on the subject.

"That's what they call second chances." Mack winked and then walked toward the kitchen door. "You better get a move on. Leave the dishes for me. I'll need something to do after you all leave." He chuckled.

Erica nodded, more than a little relieved to escape Mack's all-seeing eyes. "Thanks for letting us stay here."

"No problem. Anytime," he said as he left the kitchen.

Erica rinsed the plate and then headed outside. True to his word, Adam was there waiting. He offered her a lift up, and once settled, turned to his own horse. Ginger had been unnecessary, but she was nice for hauling all the extra supplies that made the trip a little easier.

"Thanks," Erica said, patting Joy's neck and eager to begin their journey. "I'll take the lead if you don't mind, seeing as I pretty much know the trail we're following."

Adam nodded. "Suit yourself. Just don't get too far ahead."

"Yes, sir." Erica grinned, and gave Joy a nudge, not waiting for Adam to respond. She was eager for the freedom to think, feel, and to absorb God's natural wonders that surrounded her. And Joy would make it all possible.

An hour and a half passed, and Erica's backside was feeling the hardness of the saddle. She wasn't used to riding this much without a break. It would seem the day off only let her muscles settle in and now complain more because she was back at it. The river flowed next to them, guiding her down the trail. The serene beauty beckoned Erica, and she wanted to stop. Just for a few minutes, maybe even take a couple of pictures. Twisting around in the saddle, she looked for Adam to ask him, but he was nowhere in sight.

She'd gotten ahead of him and not even noticed, so lost in her own peaceful world. A place she hadn't been in a while and was reluctant to let go. It would have been slower going for him since he was leading the other mare, and she wasn't sure how far back he might be. All the more reason for her to stop and wait.

Erica spotted a large rock outcropping and headed for it, an idea forming. Without Adam, it would be difficult at best to dismount, but she could slide off and the rock would be like a stool. The plan went off without a hitch. She eased down the rock and soon found herself on level ground. The ability to stretch was heavenly. Looking at the water and then back at the trail, another idea occurred to her. This would be the perfect time to freshen up. The water would be icy cold, but refreshing if she wiped off her face and neck. After pulling a T-shirt out of her backpack, she made her way down to the river's edge. There was a large rock that would be perfect for her to sit on so that she could soak the shirt in the river and wash off the dirt and grime.

Inching her way forward across the river pebbles, she planned out her route so as not to get her feet wet. Only a foot or so remained, and Erica leaned forward to reach for the rock. The smaller rock under her right foot rocked a bit, and she pulled back, arms outstretched, to regain her balance.

"What are you doing?" Adam thundered from behind her.

Erica swung around, lost her footing, and tumbled into the icy river water. She grabbed for the rock, trying not to let the current take her under. The water was freezing, stinging her skin, as it became harder and harder to move her arms, hands, and legs.

Moments later, Adam had her by the arm and was pulling her out of the water and into his arms, cradling her against his chest.

"*Y...you s...scared m...me,*" she said, her teeth chattering.

"What do you think you were doing?" he asked again, his voice rife with tension.

"*T...t...trying t...t...too f...freshen u...up.*"

"Great. I guess you're all clean. Now, if I can keep you from getting hypothermia, you might live to laugh about this."

"*I'll be f...f...f...fine,*" she insisted, more aware of being in his arms than of the icy chill hampering her ability to move.

Adam crossed back to the river's edge and sat her down in the grass. He hurried toward Ginger, grabbed a blanket from the saddlebag, and was back with her in an instant. He wrapped it around her, tucking the edges together. "I'll start a fire."

"*Th...thank y...you. I'm s...sorry.*" She drew the blanket tight around her body, seeking warmth to stop her chattering.

"It is what it is. We normally use a canteen with water to clean up on the trail. For this very reason. It's my fault, as I should have thought about you needing to freshen up. It would seem you didn't get the best guide, considering this happened."

It was sweet of him to take responsibility, but it was all her doing. "Not your fault. I'm sorry. You told me not to get too far ahead, and if I'd listened, I could have simply asked you. I should be fine. If you take time to build a fire, we will get behind schedule." And a promise was a promise. They simply had to get back in time for Adam to be at the fundraiser.

"Yes, but if we don't have a fire to get you dried and warm, your muscles won't cooperate much longer and then today's ride will be over before you know it," he said, his voice still crisp with tension.

Minutes later, Adam had a fire started, all without saying a word to her. She moved closer, enjoying the warmth as the flames licked higher. Adam stepped off to the side, talking on the phone. His animated gestures meant he didn't like what he was hearing, any more than he liked the delay.

If Erica had a do over, she'd take it, but she wouldn't get one. Not that she wasn't thankful Adam had been there to pull her out of the water and rescue her, but she firmly believed with all her heart that if he hadn't scared her, she wouldn't have fallen.

While Adam was occupied on the phone, Erica made her way to Joy and pulled out some dry clothes to change into. Finding privacy wasn't easy, especially with her injured leg and foot. It was times like this she wished she wasn't so embarrassed by the cane and had it with her. Perhaps she should get her own walking stick.

Moving back to the fire, she warmed her hands, holding them close to the flame. Heat slowly returned to her body, and she relaxed.

"I'm feeling better, Adam," she called out, pushing the logs for the fire apart to let it die down. She hated being the reason for another delay and wanted to get back on the trail.

He hung up the phone. "Good. There's trouble back at the house and we really need to make good time. I've got to get there tomorrow to finalize a few things before the fundraiser starts at four. Tamila, my assistant, is having a meltdown right about now."

"I'm sorry. Is there anything I can do?" Erica asked, more than a little concerned since it was all her fault he wasn't already in Juneau where he could ward off trouble. The last thing she wanted was to be responsible for the Sidekick Squad Connection to be delayed any longer.

"Stay on the trail." Adam grinned.

At least his humor had returned. He spread the embers out even more and doused the glowing embers with water.

"Got it." She laughed.

Satisfied the fire was out and cold, Adam moved to help Erica up into the saddle of her mare. They were soon back on the trail and making good progress. The ringing of Adam's phone broke the silence all around them. It would seem they were close enough for cell service again. She pulled out her phone, wanting to call her aunt and uncle to update them on what was happening. As she spoke to her aunt, it was the firm set of Adam's jaw that signaled Erica his conversation wasn't going as planned.

It was unfortunate that she'd been the one to add to his stress. For now, she'd stay out of his way and not bother him. Instead, she spent the time taking pictures and immersing herself in the beauty all around her. Joy was steady and true, handling the trail like an expert.

Soon, Erica could feel the radiant heat warming her, filling her with a renewed sense of purpose and peace. Having Adam nearby only added to her inner peace. Except the quiet solitude also gave her time to think about him and her feelings toward him.

Being with Adam the past few days showed her a side of him she remembered all too well. His love for the great outdoors and horses was like they were back in camp. Feelings Erica once thought dead and gone, were igniting to life once again.

Something she would do well to not let happen. Not given all she knew about the love he had, and still had for that matter, for his fiancé.

Chapter Fourteen

♥

The day had been long, and they hadn't covered as much ground as Adam had targeted. Thanks to Erica's crazy notion to freshen up in the freezing river. When he wasn't on the phone putting out fires for the fundraiser, his thoughts stayed centered on Erica. Luckily, he'd been able to get her out of the water quickly, as time was critical to keep hypothermia at bay.

He should have paid more attention. Pushed harder to keep up. Or made her stay behind him on the trail.

All good options, but it didn't change the outcome at this point.

Darkness would set in soon, and they still needed to eat. Adam found a suitable location for them to set up camp for the night. He held up his hand to signal the stop, and Erica pulled up alongside him.

"What's up? Did you see something?" Erica asked.

"No. Nothing more exciting than what we won't see and how cold we're going to be if we don't get settled down and get a fire started. We don't have much daylight left."

"I'm all for stopping. My backside is over and done with riding."

He led them to a wide-open spot, perfect for what they needed, and then helped her dismount.

"What can I do?"

Adam grinned. "Fix dinner."

"Do you want me to catch a salmon with my bare hands?" she asked, a teasing lilt to her voice.

Her soft smile sent a jolt of warmth to his heart. "I'm not sure you should try anything even remotely close to the water, judging by your balancing skills earlier today."

She playfully swatted his arm. "Hey, it was your fault. You were the one who came out of nowhere and scared me. Otherwise, I would have been just fine."

"Guess we'll never know. Where are you headed?" Adam asked as she started toward the river.

"To catch a fish. If I can."

"Erica, no."

"You won't even let me try? Of all the—"

"No, it's not that. When I caught the salmon with my hands, it was because there are sections of the river where thousands of salmon pass through in a small area. Easy pickings. That's not the case here where the river is really wide. I've got pork and beans for supper. You'll find the can and a loaf of bread in the saddle bags courtesy of Mack."

She nodded, but her grim expression was almost comical.

"What? Guessing pork and beans isn't your thing?" Adam chuckled.

"Nope. Can't imagine they're anyone's thing. But then, you're not anyone. You're the mountain man recluse. Probably on your menu more often than not."

"You forget...I know how to fish and cook."

"True," she conceded. "At least you aren't looking to put salmon in the beans."

"Not a bad idea," he teased.

"Gross."

"It's a joke." Adam laughed. He would have to be careful what he said around Erica, as clearly, the adventurous side of her was returning. She used to be fearless when anyone challenged her, and it would seem it was a trait she still possessed. But she wasn't a bear and wouldn't find success in her venture. Not to mention, keeping her away from the river guaranteed she would stay dry for the rest of the journey.

Adam moved off to wander the nearby woods in search of firewood. Trip after trip, until he was satisfied with the pile of wood he had stacked nearby. After organizing the wood into the traditional teepee pattern for an easy start, he lit the kindling and stepped back. Once it was good and hot with lots of glowing embers, he would push the logs out a bit to make way for the grill and pan of beans. He was mighty hungry, and the idea of a hot dinner was heavenly.

Conversation was easy with Erica. On the way out, she'd been stiff and unyielding. Now, she seemed more carefree and peaceful. At one with her surroundings. Several times, she'd gone over to where Joy was tethered to talk to the horse and stroke her long mane and back. Not for the first time, he wished he was a fly and could find out what the one-sided conversation was about.

He stirred the beans, watching as the steam rose from the pot. "Dinner will be ready in about five minutes," he called out.

"Sounds good. Actually, it smells good too. Though I can't believe I'm saying that," Erica said, hands on her hips as she shook her head.

"Hunger has a way of doing that to a person."

"I suppose," she said, returning to the fire. Without another word, Erica prepared the ground pads and sleeping bags.

Adam was impressed that she hadn't chosen to have the small pup tent set up. Her desire to see the Aurora Borealis far outweighed anything else. It was another childhood memory they shared at camp one night when he'd met up with her long after curfew. They sat and watched the spectacular light show together, hand in hand. It was a most magical moment and the moment he had fallen in love with Erica.

Stirring the beans one last time, he then ladled out a serving into a bowl and handed it to her.

"Thanks." She took a bite after blowing on them to make sure they were cool enough to eat.

"These are good." Erica dipped her bread in the juice and took a bite. "*Hmmm*. Even better."

"Glad you approve," he said, taking up his own helping, before setting the pan to the side and moving the grill in order to stoke the fire. The moonlight made it easy...and romantic.

Adam pushed back on the thought. There was no room for romance in his life. His focus was on fulfilling Natalie's dream and nothing else. Contrary to what everyone kept telling him.

"Let's play the *What am I thinking of* game," Erica said, grinning at him.

It was a game they played as kids, when life was easy. "I'm not sure I remember how to play, and it'll be time to turn in for the night soon if we're going to get an early start."

"Don't be a bore. It's a simple game and I know you remember. I'll start," she insisted, not letting him off the hook.

"Fine," he said, taking her now empty plate away and wiping them clean before placing them back in the saddle bag.

"I'm thinking of something really big," she said, when he sat back down by the fire.

Which could be about anything. "The moon," he said, going for the obvious.

"Nope. It's mostly black," she added as the second hint.

Adam frowned. "I don't have a clue." It seemed like a silly game when he knew how tired they both were.

"Come on, Adam. Play along," Erica teased, stifling a yawn.

The game wouldn't last long anyway, so he might as well humor her. "My truck."

Erica shook her head. "Nope. Good guess though. The third hint is that it lives in the sea."

"Too easy. A humpback whale." In hindsight, it should have been his first guess. When she was sixteen, she was fascinated with oceanography...especially whales. There had been plenty of conversations when she went on and on like a walking encyclopedia as she shared the information with him.

"Yes. You got it in three. I made it too easy, but I couldn't think of anything else to give as a hint."

Adam chuckled. "You always used to make it easy. I think you like guessing better."

"Maybe. Your turn."

There was no maybe about it. More and more memories of their time together flooded his brain, making it difficult to concentrate. "Let me think. *Hmmm*." He stroked his chin, wanting to come up with something she wouldn't guess. For him, he loved the challenge of outwitting her. Which wasn't easy, given how smart she was. "Okay, I'm thinking of something warm."

"The fire," she said, her eyes lit up with a warmth all of their own.

"No, but good guess. That would have been too easy. Your second hint is that it's not a living thing."

Erica continued to guess, and Adam continued to give hints. Back and forth, they joked and teased, just like when they were kids. He added wood to the fire. Erica climbed into her sleeping bag and stifled another yawn. "No fair. Your answer is too hard," she said after the tenth hint.

He could have gone on all night but opted to put an end to the game instead. "Okay, here's a dead giveaway. It was here tonight and now it's gone."

She shook her head. "I know what it is now, but I can't believe I didn't guess before. Pork and beans," she exclaimed, her smile firmly back in place.

"Right on ten." Adam chuckled. "And since it looks like you're ready to fall asleep, I'm the winner, it would seem. Ten to three."

"Oh well, there's always next time. And you're right, I'm so tired," Erica said, slipping deep into her sleeping bag and zipping it up until the whole thing covered her shoulders, but leaving her head and arms exposed.

"Tomorrow is a big day, and we need to push to get back to my place by three, so I have time to clean up before the event starts."

"Thanks for everything. I mean, I know how important tomorrow is and I'm truly grateful you helped me. I'm sorry it turned out to be a fool's errand."

"You're welcome. But Erica, I don't think the trip was a bad thing." Especially given he could have put an end to it at any moment, but that for the greater good...hadn't told her the truth. "You seem more at peace with life than you did before. I'm hoping this might all be a part of your healing process. Perhaps Joy is bringing you back some much needed joy in your heart." Seeing the positive changes in Erica is what kept him silent. That and the right moment to break the news. Tomorrow, he promised himself.

"Maybe. And you might be right, but also, spending time with you has helped. I mean, things were left unsaid when we were kids. I always wondered what happened and wondered what I would say if I met up with you again. Now I know."

Adam was glad to have cleared the air, even more so, that he wasn't the one to damage the relationship between Erica and her father. Apparently, the man had done that all on his own. "Hopefully all good."

"In truth, most of it. We were just kids, but now...I know this will sound silly...but I sort of wish we would have had our chance to make a go of things. My father ruined everything, but it doesn't change the man you've become. And spending time with you now, there's still something about you that makes me want to experience more of life and all that it offers. You've always had that effect on me."

Adam's heart swelled with emotion. "I'm also glad we had this time together. Maybe we needed this for our own healing regarding the past."

"Thank you for saying that," Erica said.

"You're welcome. One other thing, though. It's not me who makes you want to experience life. You do that on your own. It's a part of who you are...with or without me. I was just lucky enough to experience that part of you in action.

"That might be the sweetest thing you've ever said."

"It's the truth. Stop trying to close out the world, and the healing will come."

"I just wish it were possible."

"Anything is possible with faith." Adam knew based on experience and the ability to move past the pain. Erica, it would seem, might be headed in the same direction. The firelight danced across her face as he waited for her response. It was all so surreal to be here with Erica.

"I fear faith wasn't around the night of the explosion." Erica said the words ever so softly, enough so that Adam almost missed them.

But he heard, and his chest tightened, like a vice grip holding him in place. "Faith is always present.

Why don't you tell me what happened? Sharing can sometimes lighten the load." Maybe the dark of the night would give her the courage to open up to him.

She sat up, her movements jerky as though she were frustrated. Or angry. "I've shared plenty with my superiors and the review board. It's done nothing but cause me nightmares."

"Sharing with a friend is different. This is the ability to talk freely, without recourse. Try me, if you can," he added, appealing to her sense of a challenge.

Erica was silent for a long moment, as though undecided. He reached for her hand and held it tight, giving her strength. Her gaze landed on him, a distant look in her eyes, before she turned back to watch the fire.

"I was at the mess hall and stopped to talk to some of the other soldiers on the way back to the barracks. When I arrived, I figured to make good use of my free time and shine my boots in case they called for a random inspection. When I pulled open the supply closet door, I discovered one of our superiors, Sergeant Dahl, activating an explosive device. I escaped as he tried to grab me, and I ran out screaming for everyone to get out of the barracks. Soldiers are trained to react without question and there was a mass exodus from the building. I remember running for the door, and then came the explosion." Her voice had taken on a distant quality as though she were back in time.

"I didn't make it out before the doorway collapsed on my leg and foot, and one board hit my head, knocking me unconscious. By the time I came round, it was over. Soldiers and medics were scrambling to make heads or tails of what had just happened. It was then I learned three soldiers hadn't made it out of the building. Molly had been my best friend for the past three years when we landed the same deployment. And Sam, well, he was a young soldier with the weight of the world on his shoulders. We were comrades, but friends as well. And then there was Sergeant Dahl. Once I informed the Commander of what I'd seen, an investigation into Sargeant Dahl's life began. The military higher-ups aren't saying much, but it was obvious Dahl was a traitor."

Adam sucked in a deep breath, her story gut wrenching. It was a situation no one should have to experience, and losing friends compounded the problem. It was no wonder she was broken on the inside. But all the more reason she needed help. It would be too easy to get lost in misery. "I'm so sorry. It's understandable the difficult time you are having with the whole situation. It's heartbreaking losing someone you care about. I know that firsthand. But faith wasn't missing. You were guided by faith, reacted with heart and caring, and yes, training. The results could have been so much worse, but you changed the outcome. No, it wasn't perfect...but life is messy. You did the best you could, and that's all anyone can ask of you. Including yourself."

Erica wiped her eyes with the sleeve of her shirt. "That's what everyone keeps saying."

"Perhaps you should start listening...in your heart."

"Perhaps. Thanks for believing in me and trying to help. And for being such a caring friend."

"Always. Never doubt that," he said, knowing it was a solemn promise.

Erica yawned. "Goodnight, Adam."

"Goodnight, Erica." It wasn't long before he could hear her deep, even breathing. Sleep was probably the best thing for her.

He had told her he wasn't interested in having a relationship ever again, but being with Erica now made him wonder if that would always be true. Natalie was the love of his life...but was she the only one? Erica, it would seem, was also etched firmly in his heart.

So what did that say of their future? Sleep eluded him as he replayed conversations with Gilly, Mack, and even Zeke. They all seemed to think there was something more between him and Erica. Were they right?

Off in the distance, the sky began to change colors. It was like watching the heavens open up and pour the most beautiful painting one could imagine. The Aurora Borealis was making an appearance. With each passing minute, vibrant curtains of green, pink, and red blanketed the sky and intensified.

He stole a peek at the sleeping woman lying next to him. Adam was torn. Her need for sleep was great, but she would never forgive him if he didn't wake her up. Adam rolled closer and tapped somewhere in the shoulder region of the sleeping bag, where she had cocooned herself like a mummy. "Erica, wake up."

Adam tapped harder when she didn't budge. "Erica, wake up," he said, louder this time.

"Adam? What's wrong?" Erica asked, her voice crackly with sleep.

"Nothing. It's what's right. Poke your head out and look at the sky."

Erica unzipped the sleeping bag and glimpsed up at the sky in the direction he pointed. She instantly sat up. "The Aurora Borealis," she exclaimed, her breath leaving wisps of warm moisture that floated away into the night.

Adam nodded. "Absolutely. And beautifully on display this evening."

"Breathtaking. It's like a light show from God. The swirls seem to dance across the sky. What a perfect ending to the day. Even the stars are twinkling in merriment. Thank you for waking me up. I wouldn't have wanted to miss this for anything," she crooned.

"My pleasure. Anything for you, Erica."

"Why are you still awake?" she asked.

He shrugged. "Couldn't sleep."

"Any particular reason?" she pressed.

"Thinking about life. And you," he admitted, though he wasn't sure it was his best idea.

"Me?" she asked, moving closer. Adam tossed the extra blanket around their shoulders as they watched the miracle unfold in the sky.

"Us," he added, clarifying what he meant.

"Do you think we would have made it work?" she asked, her voice barely above a whisper.

"There's no way to know, but if I was a betting man...I would have bet on it."

Erica turned to face him, her mouth just inches away. Adam leaned forward, the move as natural as breathing. Pleased Erica didn't pull back, he let the magic of the moment carry him the rest of the way. His lips met hers and it felt right. Adam pulled her closer, his eyes closed, wanting to feel the magic of holding Erica in his arms again.

When she pulled back to look at him, the questioning expression in her eyes grounded him. "Adam?"

"Sorry. It felt right." The problem was...he wasn't sorry. And it did feel right. Too right, and it scared him.

"I agree, but what..."

"I don't know. Let's just enjoy the light show. Perhaps tomorrow, after the fundraiser, we can sort through what this means. I just can't afford to be distracted right now."

"Okay. And Adam, I understand about Natalie."

"Thank you." Now if only *he* could understand about Natalie.

Having kissed Erica, he couldn't take it back. But what of Natalie? It didn't seem right. The kiss had only confused things more because he didn't want to take it back. In fact, part of him wanted a repeat performance.

Chapter Fifteen

♥

The ringing in Erica's ears wouldn't stop. She was so tired, but the noise brought her out of a deep sleep. She unzipped the sleeping bag and sat up. She spotted Adam's phone on the rock nearby as the ringing sound pierced the air again. It struck her as odd, as she hadn't even realized they had cell service again, considering they were still half a day's ride from town.

Adam must have left it there in the dark last night, but where was he now? She scanned their makeshift campsite, noting his rolled up sleeping bag strapped onto Jasmine already.

She slid out of the sleeping bag, tapped her boots upside down in case any bugs decided to sleep there, and then slid them on her feet. She stood, determined to make the phone stop ringing. Whoever was calling clearly had no intention of stopping until Adam answered. *Maureen.*

Erica debated what to do, wondering where Adam had gone off to. The phone stopped ringing, but her relief was short-lived as the shrill sound started in again. This time, Erica hit the answer button in order to silence the call.

"Hello?" Erica said tentatively, unsure of the sanity of answering Adam's phone.

"Who's this? I demand to speak to Adam Landon," the woman's sharp tones like nails on a chalkboard.

"My name is Erica Carter. I'm not sure where Adam is at the moment. He's probably washing up in the river. May I have him call you back?" She had never met the woman and so far, didn't have a problem with her. Not enough to be rude anyway.

"Call me back? Hardly. Find him now. He has no business out there with you. What kind of woman are you, anyway? Traipsing off with another woman's fiancé out to God knows where. It's simply not right. How dare you try to steal him from my Natalie and tarnish her memory," Maureen snapped.

Except now the woman had crossed a line. "Ma'am, he's a wilderness guide. That's what I hired him for. Nothing more, nothing less." Well, except for the kiss they shared. And the fact he was doing this for free.

"*Hmmphh*. I wasn't born yesterday. Have you found him yet?"

No. Erica scanned the area again, praying for Adam's return. "I...actually, he's coming up the trail now. Hold on," she said, keeping the phone at her side to avoid the tirade the woman was unleashing, and more than a little relieved to see him.

"What's going on?" Adam asked, glancing down at the phone in her hand.

"It's Maureen," she said in a low voice. "Not a happy camper and demanding to speak to you. Sorry if I shouldn't have answered, but it kept ringing and ringing, and I was worried there was an emergency."

"It's fine," he said, his crisp tone the exact opposite. Adam took the phone and moved off toward the horses, clearly seeking privacy.

"What's up, Maureen?" she heard him ask.

Erica could hear his part of the conversation, the morning air still and calm. He was silent for a few minutes and Erica knew Adam was getting an earful. She'd had a tiny taste of the woman's nastiness and preferred not to suffer more of it.

Part of the problem was that Maureen wasn't entirely wrong. She and Adam had been alone for most of the journey, and it was bound to raise a few eyebrows. Given tonight's fundraiser and program's grand opening next month, the timing couldn't have been worse.

"You can't put a stop to the Sidekick Squad, Maureen. We've been over this time and time again. This is what Natalie wanted. Why can't you understand I'm trying to honor your daughter's legacy? It's no more than you should be doing." Adam was angry, his voice loud and clear.

Enough so that Erica could hear the love in Adam's voice when he mentioned Natalie. Last night's magical kiss was a fleeting moment in time. She'd been giddy like she was back in high school, but this time was different. Older now, the feelings in her heart went far beyond what she experienced as a young girl.

If anything, she could admit her feelings had been more along the lines of a high school crush, but what did that say about now? The worst thing she could do was fall in love with a man who had 'emotionally unavailable' written in every pore of his body.

Except for last night's kiss.

Erica needed to forget about the experience they shared, including the kiss. She'd come a long way with Joy and Adam by her side, but there was more healing to be done. Talking with Adam had been a blessing in disguise. She realized it was time to take control of her life and fight back to find happiness. *Without Adam.* Her military buddies would have wanted her to keep living. It was something they all talked about in the wee hours of the morning, when they shared their deepest fears, joy, and regrets.

Adam returned to her side, the lines of tension deeply etched across his forehead.

"What's wrong? She was quick to read me the riot act for being here with you. I'm sorry if I caused you any trouble." Her heart ached for Adam. He was trying so hard to do what was right.

"I'm sorry you were at the receiving end of her bitterness and grief. She's lost without her daughter and still acts like Natalie's coming back. Maureen needs grief counseling, but I doubt she'll get it. That would require facing the fact her daughter's not coming back." Adam ran a hand through his hair, something he did often when he was stressed.

"Well, what does she want this time? Other than us not to have taken this trip, that is," Erica asked.

Adam shook his head. "She was just letting off steam, amongst other things."

"Other things?"

"Yes, it would seem she may have finally found the loophole she needs to shut me down. Maureen is good friends with one of the town council members and convinced her I don't have the proper license to hold this fundraiser or start a business."

"Is she right?" Erica asked.

"Yes, and no. I've got the proper state licensing, but it would seem there's an archaic law on the county books that Maureen discovered that would require me to have a county license as well. I've got to see what I can do to fix this." He checked his watch. "In eight hours or less. We need to get a move on."

Erica couldn't imagine anyone going to such great lengths to stop something so beneficial. "Sounds ridiculous if no one even knew it existed until Maureen dredged it up from who knows where. Is there anything I can do to help?"

"Pray. Getting on the county docket for a hearing could take months. And then there's no guarantee I get a majority vote with Maureen stirring up trouble."

"For sure. And Adam, it will be okay. I'm sure of it. Do whatever it takes. I believe in you, and I believe the Sidekick Squad Connection is a valuable resource for kids."

"Thank you. That means a lot to me to hear I have your support. I can use all the help I can get. I figured a quick breakfast was in order so that we can be on our way without delay. Hence, the peanut butter and jelly sandwich quick fix. Sorry," he said, as he handed her a sandwich.

"It's fine. At least it's strawberry jelly." Erica laughed, hoping to return Adam's good humor.

"There is that." Adam poured her a cup of coffee and held it out to her. "I'll start cleaning up the site and packing the horses so we can be on the trail by eight at the latest."

Erica watched Adam in action for a bit, going over and over in her head the events of last night. The Aurora Borealis had been spectacular, but Adam's kiss had it beat ten times over. The downside to it all, that he didn't even want to talk about it. *For now*. Secret code for never in her books. She was an expert on evading discussions she didn't want to have.

"Time to roll," Adam called out.

Erica tossed her clothes from yesterday in the backpack and headed for where the horses were tied. Adam helped her up, and Erica settled in the saddle, the ache in her thighs and butt causing a slight groan from the pain. She would have thought by now her body would be accustomed to riding, but perhaps this was a bit more than easing back into something.

Adam hoisted himself into the saddle, clicked his heels against Jasmine's flanks, and took off, leading Ginger down the trail, leaving Erica to follow.

They rode in silence. Well, for her anyway. Adam spent hours on the phone with one person or another, trying to bring about a last-minute miracle to save the fundraiser and the program.

Erica couldn't help but feel sorry for him. Having to fight the one woman he should have been able to count on had to make the situation that much worse. They were both struggling with the loss of someone they loved, but each had found a different way to cope. Adam's determination to continue was proof of his love for Natalie. Something Erica could never compete with, nor would she want to. But being second best to someone else was never her thing and never would be. Her parents taught her that lesson when her father cheated on her mother.

Crossing the river slowed them down, but at least it was passable this time. Adam's tension seemed to multiply with each passing minute. At noon, he stopped to give the horses a break and for lunch.

"Any luck?" she asked, knowing the answer, judging from the firm set of his jaw.

Adam shook his head. "No, but I have an idea."

"I'll take care of the horses and fix us sandwiches, and you take care of business," she said, taking the reins from him.

"Thanks, Erica. I owe you one."

"No problem. And consider us even since you did this entire trip for me."

"Thanks. We have no time to lose. The extra crossing time has set us back more than I wanted. By the time we get to the house, the fundraiser will have already started." Adam got back on the phone and Erica couldn't help but hear bits and pieces of the conversation, but only his side of the call. He was quite convincing, to say the least.

When he hung up, his smile told the story. It was the first one of the day and it was a welcome sight. "I got the license, or I'll have it in about an hour anyway. A friend of mine is the judge's son-in-law, and he could pull some strings, even on a weekend. He's going to have it delivered to Tamila."

"That's wonderful news. I'm so sorry we are running late. I hope you'll forgive me, as I know how much you needed to be there." Erica resisted the urge to hug Adam, wanting to share in his joy, but also knowing she ruined this event for him.

"It's okay. But we should get a move on. I'll call the council president and let her know that Maureen's attempt to stop this has failed. Again."

Soon they were back on the trail and closing the distance to Adam's place. They picked up the pace, going as fast as possible, while erring to the side of caution for the horse and rider. Of course, the third horse didn't help expedite matters. It put an end to any conversation until they came to a clearing in the fields and Erica spotted Adam's house in the far distance.

Adam suddenly reined in Jasmine, his phone glued to his ear. He shook his head and let out a deep breath.

"What is it, Adam?" she asked, pulling alongside him.

"Tamila called me, and Maureen showed up at the fundraiser. Everyone's already there and she's raising cain."

"Then go! Don't wait for me. I can see your house from here, so I know where I'm going. I'll take Ginger with me. You can get there a lot quicker without us."

"Thanks, Erica." He untied Ginger and handed her the rope. And like a bolt of lightning, horse and rider were off and running at full speed. She wasn't that good of a rider yet, but perhaps one day soon, she would be...with Joy.

Chapter Sixteen

♥

Adam drew Jasmine to a halt, barely taking the seconds needed to tie the mare to the post. He would have to come back out at the first possible moment to take care of the horses, but the tirade going on inside his home took precedence. They were a half an hour late, and Tamila was beside herself, worried that people would start leaving unless he could do something about Maureen.

He never expected Natalie's mother would have the audacity to show up, given everything that had gone down between them. In fact, she'd been adamant she wouldn't dream of stepping foot in his house. The only thing that had changed was that Maureen's last-ditch effort to stop his plans had failed. She was here to make trouble, and he was the only one who could step up and have her removed from the event...effectively anyway, since it was his home where she was technically trespassing and causing a disturbance.

Preferably before she left a sour taste in everyone's mouth and ruined the whole affair.

He took the steps two at a time, pulled open the door, and raced inside. People were in the hallway, shocked expressions on their faces. They pointed toward the living room, not that he needed directions. Adam could hear Maureen yelling at anyone who would listen.

A friend clapped him on the back, encouraging Adam as he started forward, ready to take on the riotous woman. Stepping through the double door entry that was wide open, he pulled up short and stopped. At the front of the room, larger than life, Natalie's smiling face stared back at him from the video screen, her voice like she was right here in the room. Adam sucked in a deep breath, trying to regain control of his emotions. He hadn't planned on the video having such an effect...at least not on him. Everything came back to him in a rush.

Tears filled his eyes. Seconds passed before he realized Maureen had grown quiet. Someone was sobbing, their outward grief quieting the entire room. He moved forward, only to discover the crier was none other than Maureen. She was sitting in a chair, her eyes glued to the screen, her hands stretched outward as though the need to touch her daughter would bring her back. Maureen's shoulders were slumped, the spindly woman no longer a fortress. Instead, she was a grieving mother mourning the loss of her daughter.

Adam moved forward, the overwhelming need to comfort Maureen taking hold. Reaching her side, he held out his arms. After only seconds of hesitation, she stood and stepped into his embrace. Silently sobbing, the woman shook in his arms as the video played, Natalie holding court over the entire room.

Even Maureen turned back to the screen and listened to her daughter. Natalie talked about her dream. The vision she had to help children find outlets of happiness that could make a difference in a child's life. The Sidekick Squad Connection was her baby. Wherever Natalie went, people loved her. Loved her gentle spirit and willingness to help others.

Maureen moved forward, lightly touching the screen with her hand. Then she kissed her fingertips and touched Natalie's lips reverently. "Natalie. Natalie. Natalie. My dearest daughter. I love you and miss you."

Someone handed Maureen a tissue. Adam wiped his eyes with the back of his hand. Several people moved forward and enveloped her in their arms. Minutes passed, and then Maureen searched the crowd, her tear-filled eyes landing on Adam. She returned to his side, surprising him when she reached up to hug him.

"I'm sorry, Adam," she said through her tears.

"I understand. Truly. Natalie was an amazing woman. All I want is for people to remember her and the joy she brought to others. There was no way I couldn't honor her by finishing what she started. The Sidekick Squad Connection is her legacy of love."

"I understand that now. I'm so sorry. This just makes it all so final. And the idea of seeing her name and having her memory constantly brought up scared me. I wanted to keep her all to myself, but I was wrong. Thank you for honoring my daughter. It wasn't just my loss, but everyone she knew who loved her. Including you. Her kindness and memory will be forever in the hearts of the children she helps, thanks to you."

"Thanks to us, Maureen. You're Natalie's mother, and she became the woman she was because of you. And now, every child she helps will be because of her dream. Every life touched will be made better because of her dedication to the cause."

"Yes. I see that. Can you forgive me?" Maureen asked.

"There's nothing to forgive. You were struggling as a grieving mother. No one has a rule book on what grief looks like from one person to the next. I'm just happy you've made peace in your heart. Natalie would have wanted you to be a part of all this," he said, pointing to everyone in the room as they continued to watch the video.

The last image of Natalie filled the screen, her smile warm and engaging. The cheers and tears of everyone present were overwhelming. The event would be a success, and Natalie's legacy would finally begin.

"I do have one question. Make that two." Maureen actually smiled through her tears.

"What's that?"

"If I want to make a donation to the cause, who should I write the check out to?"

"The Sidekick Squad Connection Foundation for Children. And thank you so much. What's your other question?" Adam couldn't believe the turn of events, but it was a genuine miracle.

"Can I be one of the first mentors for a child in need?" Maureen asked.

"Absolutely. What a blessing and an honor." Adam meant every word, but also knew there were lots of people signed up for the same thing. The community had opened their arms to the program, and the list was extensive.

"You have shown how much you loved my daughter, and I don't believe anyone could have honored her more than you have. Thank you, Adam."

"You're welcome. I loved Natalie with all my heart, and I miss her dearly."

"Yes, I don't doubt that all. And I'm sorry about what I said to you earlier today. About being with that other woman. I'm sure it meant nothing."

Adam nodded, suddenly remembering Erica. There wasn't much to say in response to Maureen's comment, because he wasn't sure 'nothing' was a good word to describe the newest twist in their friendship. In fact, the kiss made him realize that he and Erica might just have a second chance at love. And he wasn't looking to run from it.

Now that the fundraiser looked as though it would be a tremendous success, Tamila would be promoted to program director and take over running the daily details. Her dedication this past year had proven her quite capable for the job. As for Adam, all that was left was the grand opening, and mentoring children along the way now and then.

Chapter Seventeen

♥

It hadn't been easy dismounting from Joy, but the mare held steady. It worked well enough that Erica slid slowly off on the left side with both feet, gingerly putting her weight on the left foot. Learning to adapt her moves would always be a part of her future, as the doctor had warned her that even after her ankle healed, there would be times of aching from the scar tissue.

Once in the house, she had made her way down the hall to the great room where throngs of people were gathered around. She'd caught the last few minutes of the video and knew instantly why everyone loved Natalie. The gorgeous brunette had a smile like the sun and was like a breath of fresh air and a powerhouse of energy. *Like a modern-day Princess Diana.*

Adam was off to the side, hugging a woman whose features appeared similar to Natalie. Erica figured she was the infamous Maureen...but the raving troublemaker of earlier was nowhere to be seen. She wasn't sure what happened, but knew for certain a miracle had occurred. What a blessing for Adam and Natalie.

Not wanting to intrude on the affair, Erica slipped back out the door. She wandered through the house, curious about Adam and the man he had become. Wildlife paintings hung on the wall with wood frames. The soothing greens, rusts, and cream-colored accents throughout the place were like stepping into an indoor forest of peace and tranquility. The wood furniture was blocky, but finely crafted. She ran a hand over the smooth wood, admiring its beauty. As she moved down the hall to inspect the photographs that hung there, it was like opening the door to the past ten years of Adam's life.

Pictures of Natalie and Adam. Pictures of him riding a horse. Pictures of him as a young man...the Adam she remembered.

Erica moved back through the hall, deciding to wait for Adam in the kitchen. Glancing at the photos yet again, she smiled. In the kitchen, she helped herself to the coffee; the aroma filling the air and letting her know it was hot and ready to drink. She sat down to wait, relieved to be off her foot and leg. Sipping her coffee, something nagged at her brain, but she couldn't quite figure it out.

She mentally replayed her walk-through Adam's house, but nothing made sense. Giving up on figuring it out, she opted to tend to the horses. All three of them needed brushing down, fresh water, and hay. It was the least she could do to help Adam, considering all he had done for her.

Outside, she untied Joy's reins from the hitching post and started toward the barn. Suddenly, she stopped. The image of Adam walking a horse toward the barn that hung in the hall flashed in her head. Except the horse she imagined was Joy. Her brain was playing tricks, but the image wouldn't let go. Erica turned around and headed back to the house, tying Joy to the post. Thinking Adam was riding Joy in the photo was a silly jump to make, but it stuck hard enough so that she needed to prove it to herself that she was imagining things.

Except she wasn't imagining anything. There was no denying what she saw in the photo standing in front of it. Joy. Adam and Joy were a team. Adam was Joy's previous owner, which also made him Erica's benefactor. No wonder Zeke and Mack looked at Adam funny when she started asking questions. The entire trip was a lie and completely unnecessary. The people in town obviously knew the truth as well. *Did her aunt and uncle?*

The very idea was mind-boggling. They had all made a fool of her.

Adam the most.

How could he do this to her?

She took the photo off the wall, prepared to confront Adam. It was neither the time nor the place, but she wasn't staying in this house a moment longer. In fact, she hoped she never saw Adam Landon again. Erica laid the photograph on the table in the foyer, desperate to leave.

Talk about a lucky save. She had been fooled about Joy, and fooled into thinking Adam might care. The truth was obvious. Natalie was his dream woman and Erica would forever be the friend. But what kind of friend lies about something so important?

Erica headed outside, needing fresh air. Joy snorted in recognition and stamped her feet, refusing to be ignored. She moved to stroke the mare's long neck and nose, needing to be comforted. Joy was real, and it would seem the only thing real in Erica's life at the moment.

Except even the mare belonged to Adam. Technically, she was Erica's now, but it wasn't a gift she wanted. *Until now.*

"What should I do, Joy?" The mare nuzzled against her shoulder as though in understanding. "I love you and I want to keep you, but I don't see how it's possible." Joy whinnied. Tears filled Erica's eyes and ran down her face. Joy was her newfound friend. Why did everything good have to be taken away from her?

Though in this instance, Joy wasn't being taken away. More a case that Erica needed to return her based on the principle of the situation. She'd gone searching for the previous owner to return the mare, and now she had found the benefactor. *Nothing changed.*

But in the end, Erica was still on the losing end of Joy, but also of the joy in her heart.

"I thought things were going well. I mean, I finally felt like the dark cloud over my head was being lifted...and now this. I'm so sorry, girl. But I've got to go. I'll miss you so much. You'll also have a piece of my heart. Thank you for all you have done to help me."

Joy nuzzled her shoulder again, pushing her off balance. The mare understood her emotions far too well and Erica's heart was breaking.

But everything around her was a lie. She was nothing more than the injured former military Veteran who needed a pity party. At least to their way of thinking.

No more. It was time to take back control of her life.

She walked Joy to the barn and fed her one of the apple treats from the basket Adam kept just inside the door. After brushing Joy down and giving her feed and water, she closed the stall door. With one last hug and one last look, Erica headed outside. The sun had gone behind the clouds, a perfect reflection of how she felt at the moment.

Erica pulled out her phone and called for a ride to take her back to her aunt and uncle's. While she waited, she moved the other horses to the barn, making sure they were taken care of. No matter how much she hurt, the horses had done nothing wrong and deserved attention.

The driver arrived shortly after she finished, and fifteen minutes later dropped her off. She hauled her belongings to the porch and dropped them on a rocker.

Pulling open the door, she stormed into the house. "Aunt Mary," she hollered.

"In here," her aunt called out from the kitchen.

Erica ignored the pain in her foot and charged straight into the kitchen to confront her aunt.

"I didn't expect you here—"

"Did you know about Joy?" Erica demanded.

Her aunt's face drained of color, her guilty expression more than a little revealing. "Know what?"

"That Joy was a gift from Adam." She wouldn't leave any opportunity for her aunt to fudge the facts.

"Well, that's not technically correct. But yes, I knew, and I wanted to tell you. I promise. But Adam had his reasons for not telling you, and admittedly, I understood where he was coming from in not telling you. You were a shadow of yourself when you arrived, and it broke my heart."

Erica shook her head. "It all still comes down to lying." How could her aunt even try to justify the situation?

"Perhaps, but with a cause. You really should talk to Adam. It's his story to tell. Not to mention, if you knew Adam was Joy's previous owner, you would have returned her straight away. Because you didn't, I see a new woman standing in front of me. Someone who is in control of her life again. Without Joy and your journey, who's to say if you'd still be hiding behind a wall of fear to live life to the fullest again?"

Erica leaned against the counter, arms crossed over her chest. The whole situation was overwhelming, and she wished she could wave a magic wand and escape from it all. "You might be right, but a lie is a lie. I can't trust people who lie."

"Please forgive us, dear," her aunt pleaded.

"I'm sure in time, I will. But for now, I'm leaving. I need space to figure out my life. *Alone*. I've left Joy at Adam's place." It was a snap decision, but it felt like the right one. *Mostly*. Other than the ache in her heart, that is.

"Where will you go?" her aunt asked, concern written across her face.

Erica shrugged. "I don't know yet. But I know I'm not up to dealing with Adam or anyone else who will laugh at my stupidity."

"No one is laughing. Adam went through some tough times. Joy was such a blessing. And yes, the whole town knew Joy was his, but no one doubted his gift and the love behind the gift. Love sometimes has a way of clouding someone's judgment when it comes to trying to help them. Which is the same thing your uncle and I were trying to do."

"Maybe so. I just need space."

Her aunt moved closer, placing one hand over Erica's. "There's something you should consider before you take the ultimate step and leave."

"What's that?"

"Joy. You have formed a bond with the mare. Your eyes light up when you mention her name. What about her loss when you leave?"

"The same could be said about Adam."

"Except Adam is still around and sees Joy. Joy gained a friend. She didn't lose one."

It was true, Erica would miss Joy, but it's not like she could take her anywhere and provide for her.

Not if she was leaving town. It was better this way. And she'd already said her goodbyes to Joy.

And truth be told, she didn't need Adam. Perhaps had wanted him back in her life...but didn't need him. Love had a stupid way of making you feel things you didn't want to feel. Hopefully, in no time at all, she'd forget every emotion she ever felt toward Adam and get on with her life. There was assuredly a grain of truth in what her aunt said about Adam, and therein lay the problem.

He'd done what he did to help her, not hurt her. It was only her pride that was hurt when she'd been made to look like a fool. And pride cometh before the fall. If healing was the endgame, then God, Joy, and Adam had all managed to bring her around. She couldn't hate Adam for wanting to help her. In fact, God talks about forgiveness in the Bible, and this is one of those times she needed to pay attention...and put into action.

Forgive Adam. Yes.

Stick around town...not a chance.

Chapter Eighteen

♥

A couple of hours later, the fundraiser was drawing to a close. Earlier, Adam had searched the living room for Erica, but hadn't seen her anywhere. A second quick check confirmed the horses had been taken care of, and when he spoke to Erica next, he would be sure to thank her. He was surprised she had disappeared without a word, but then perhaps the event was uncomfortable for her to join, given that the entire thing was based on a tribute to Natalie. After his thank you speech and the announcement of the huge financial success, he left Tamila and Maureen in charge.

Adam couldn't wait to share the good news with Erica, but he needed to find her first. He searched the house, but she was nowhere to be found. "Have you seen Erica anywhere, Tamila?"

His assistant shrugged. "Not lately. I mean, the last I saw her was not long after you arrived, but then she vanished, and I haven't seen her since."

Several people joined them, but Adam would let Tamila field the questions, considering she was the newly named program director. His priority was to find Erica. "Okay, thanks. I'll check the barn. Maybe she's out there with the horses. It wouldn't surprise me," he added with a grin.

It was with such a sense of freedom that he headed for the barn, light on his feet and feeling the joy in his heart. The Sidekick Squad Connection was in full-speed ahead mode, and the first mentor-child connections would be matched up and set for the grand opening next month. Of course, he couldn't have done it without all the volunteers and Tamila. They had been a Godsend to make Natalie's dream come true.

"Erica," he called out as he entered the barn. She didn't answer, and he moved to check the stalls, finding all three horses exactly where they should be, and with plenty of food and water, and the tack all put away.

"Erica," he called out again, but there was no sign of her. Maybe she was bored and had called for a ride, but he was slightly put off by the fact she hadn't said goodbye. He was sure they had moved beyond the past and were friends again. *Maybe more than friends*. And now that he was free to move on with his life and think of the future, he needed to talk to Erica and test the waters. Needed to see how she felt about him. Ever since Zeke brought up the idea of loving again, Adam hadn't been able to get the possibility completely out of his head.

Did he love Erica?

Did she love him?

Adam dialed Erica's number, but it rolled to voicemail. The urgency to talk to her hit him square in the gut. His earlier elation dwindled. Her silence worried him, but he couldn't fathom why. Call it a sixth sense, but something was wrong. Back in the house, he said some last goodbyes to the last folks leaving. He needed to get cleaned up and go see Erica, the need to talk to her overwhelming.

Closing the front door, he stepped back into the foyer, his gaze dropping to the table. One of his framed photos had been tossed carelessly on the table. Moving closer, he recognized the picture of himself...and Joy.

Erica. It was the only explanation.

If this was the reason for her disappearing act and silence, Adam knew he was in deep trouble. The plan had been to tell her the truth before they got back to the house, but then everything had gone haywire, and he didn't get the chance.

Initially, he had kept quiet because he wasn't the one who gave her Sundancer's Joy. Hadn't even known Gilly was going to deliver the horse. But he knew who the horse belonged to, and Erica might never forgive him for not telling her.

This wasn't like not telling her about her father's decree when they were still in high school and in the throes of a crush. But to tell her would have put an end to the healing process with Joy. And until now, he'd always fully believed it was worth her alienation to help her recover from the trauma. But the depth of his feelings had grown, and losing her seemed vitally wrong. Like he would lose a part of himself.

Pulling his phone from the back pocket of his jeans, he pulled up the text messaging app.

Adam: Where are you?

Erica: My aunt's place. How dare you make a fool out of me? I know about Joy. Leave me alone. I don't need you to figure out my life. I took care of the horses. Joy's your responsibility now.

Adam: I'm sorry. My intentions were to help, that's all. And I didn't gift you Joy, Gilly did. Please, we need to talk.

Erica: No. We. Don't.

Adam: Please Erica, give me a chance to explain.

Erica. No. There's nothing to talk about. You lied and I'm leaving town. For good. I don't belong here.

Except she belonged here...with him. A good-bye, see-you-never-again text wasn't happening, not when he cared about her as much as he did. When he was in high school, he let her father warn him off. But this time, he wouldn't bow out of the picture without a fight. As for Erica, running is what she did best. After high school, she enlisted in the military. And now, she was looking to run again. *From him.* Except this time, he wouldn't let her go. And he knew in his heart why. *Love.*

Natalie would always hold a special place in his heart, but clearly God was giving him another chance at happiness. Had he blown it? Or would

Erica give him the opportunity to prove they were meant to be together?

Two different women, both worthy of a special forever kind of love. But it was up to Erica to trust her heart and believe in herself and that she was worthy of love. Adam was in love for the last time of his life, and he wouldn't stand by and let Erica slip away.

He climbed in his truck and headed for the Carter place. His brain was racing in ten different directions, but all of them centered on Erica. Over and over, he tried to come up with the right words to let her know how he felt.

I think there's something between us.

Maybe we should be together.

I feel something for you and want to give us a chance.

Don't leave.

Everything sounded lame to his way of thinking.

I love you.

Perhaps coming right out and saying the words was best. Because he knew in his heart that he loved Erica. After that, the rest would be up to her.

If only she would give him the chance to tell her and explain about Joy.

Adam parked the truck in front of the house and made his way to the porch. He rapped sharply on the front door, and seconds later, Mary greeted him, a concerned expression on her face. She shook her head, lips pursed.

"Is Erica here?" he asked.

"She is. I'm sorry, Adam, but she told me she didn't want to see or talk to you. I must abide by her decision. I know you meant well, but she's too upset to see past the lie."

"Except I never lied. I've already told you I didn't know Gilly gave her the horse. And I can't apologize or explain what happened if she doesn't talk to me."

Mary stepped out onto the porch. "I understand. Truly. But I've already shaken her confidence in our own relationship by not telling her what I knew from the beginning, and I won't do anything to make the situation worse."

"Please...I've got to talk to her." He wasn't above begging.

"I'm sorry, Adam. It's probably best if you leave."

He let out a deep sigh. Adam hadn't planned on Erica ignoring him all together. "But—"

"No buts. The only thing I can tell you is that she plans on catching the noon train tomorrow."

Something else he hadn't expected. "Where's she going?"

Mary suddenly looked years older, her forlorn expression filled with sadness. "I'm not sure. She hasn't told me yet."

Adam leaned in and dropped a kiss on her cheek. "Thanks for the information and all of your help with the program. You missed the grand finale, but Maureen Vincent is now one of our biggest supporters."

"What wonderful news. I'd love to hear all about it sometime, but right now isn't a good time." She flashed a quick peek back through the screen door, as if to make sure they weren't overheard. "And Adam, good luck. With Erica," she added, her voice so low he barely heard the words.

"Thanks. It would seem I'm going to need a lot of luck topped off with loads of prayer."

Mary nodded before moving inside and closing the door. Adam stood there, wondering what to do next. And he had less than twenty-four hours to figure it out, because there was no way Erica was getting on that train tomorrow without knowing he loved her.

Chapter Nineteen

♥

The following morning, Erica came downstairs, lugging her suitcase. After making a couple of trips back and forth to her room, her foot was aching, but not nearly as much as her heart. From the upstairs bedroom window, she'd watched Adam leave yesterday. It took every ounce of staying power not to run after him. Especially when she noticed his slumped shoulders, as though his normal air of confidence deserted him.

But it was all too much to contend with. His lie was big. But bigger still was the love he still had for Natalie. Leaving simply made it easier for Erica to hide behind the wall she had erected. A wall meant to protect her broken heart.

Her aunt guessed at the crux of the problem, but Erica refused to confirm or deny her comments. Her uncle, on the other hand, was less delicate about the entire matter. He thought she was running away and should stick around and talk to Adam. But what did men know about hearts and emotions and self-preservation?

It had been a long night, filled with tears. And her firm resolve this morning was to leave and not look back. Make her own happiness. Without the military, and without Adam. She loved Adam with all her heart. Probably had since she was sixteen. But she didn't want to be his second choice. Second best in love.

Not to mention he'd made a fool of her. Yes, he was trying to help...which was sweet in its own way. But it stung. Especially when she thought back over everything that had happened between them. Things she'd said and done, and all the while Adam knew Joy was his horse and that he was the benefactor. Any hope of trust had been destroyed the minute she discovered his duplicity.

Her uncle came through the front door just as she moved to pull it open. "Erica, you sure you don't want to change your mind?" he asked, picking up her suitcases and moving them to the front porch. "Not just because your aunt and I will miss you, for that's a given. It's been nice having you here."

Erica let out a deep sigh. "I can't, Uncle John. I'll visit again after I figure out what I'm going to do with my life and where I'm going to live. I need to make my own way in the world to get strong again."

"But what will you do?"

She shrugged. It was the same question she had asked herself a hundred times since leaving Adam's place. "I've enjoyed riding again, so maybe I could get a job at a ranch." She shrugged. "Maybe cooking or something where my foot's not a problem but that they'll let me ride the horses occasionally."

Her uncle nodded. "Sounds like your mind's made up and that you've given this some thought. I've got a friend, name's Henry Jones. Lives over in Willow. He's got a nice ranch and might need an extra hand. You should look him up and tell him I sent you."

Finally, she might actually catch a break and have something concrete for a new direction. "Thank you, Uncle John." Erica moved to hug him. Clearly, her uncle had accepted her decision.

She didn't want to leave at odds with her aunt and uncle...or the whole town, for that matter.

Just Adam. He was the real problem in all of this.

Uncle John checked his watch. "Your aunt should be back any minute. She had to run an errand in town. I'll get all this luggage loaded and then we'll run you into the train station."

"Thank you." She followed him outside and moved to stand by the car while she waited.

Less than five minutes later, her aunt arrived. "Sorry, my errand took a little longer than I expected. You've still got forty-five minutes before the noon train arrives, so no worries there." Gone was her sullen aunt, her radiant smile and upbeat attitude downright jovial.

And confusing.

Maybe her aunt was happy she was leaving...it was the only explanation Erica could come up with. "That's fine. But we should get going."

Her aunt nodded. "Absolutely. Don't want to be late and miss that train."

Now Erica was positive her aunt was looking to get rid of her, and it stung. What happened to trying to convince her to stay? Or that she was making a huge mistake. Something changed, and it was yet another emotional hit that Erica could have done without.

They climbed into the truck, her aunt sliding into the middle. Her uncle shifted into reverse, backed up, then headed down the driveway and toward town.

"So where are you headed, Erica?" her aunt asked, intent on making small talk to break the silence.

"Uncle John mentioned Willow. It's only an hour from here, and I remember it being a picturesque town, so I thought I would start there."

"Not as nice as Juneau, but it is a quaint area."

"Glad to hear you're going to take me up on the suggestion. Keep us posted," her uncle said.

They turned the corner, only to discover the entire street was filled with people. It reminded her of the day she'd come back to Juneau and discovered they were holding a welcome party for her. An event met with mixed emotions. "What's going on, Uncle John?" Erica leaned forward in her seat to get a better view as she asked the question. Her uncle slowed the truck, throngs of people in the street blocking their way.

"I don't rightly know," he said, shifting the truck into park. "Perhaps we should go find out because we are still a bit far from the station to walk with all your luggage."

"Just be patient, both of you," her aunt countered, surprising them both.

At what point was she impatient? "We are being patient. It's like they are having a sit in."

Uncle John shut off the truck and slid out, her aunt hot on his heels. Erica opened the passenger door and exited the truck to follow them, curious about what all the commotion was about.

If she had to walk the rest of the way, she would, provided, of course, her uncle could bring along her luggage and folks let them pass through. The cutoff for buying a ticket was fifteen minutes before the train arrived, which left little time to get to the ticket counter.

She started forward, just as the group of people parted. Their grinning smiles made no sense, but she didn't have time to question why. The train station came into view, and she wasn't about to pass up the opportunity to slip through the crowd. Erica turned to see if her aunt and uncle were following, more than a little relieved to see them closing the distance.

As she turned back, Erica ran headlong into a broad-chested man, which halted her progress. She looked up, squinting against the sun.

Adam.

And Joy.

At a loss for words, Erica's heart swelled with joy and tears trickled down her face. Adam was resplendent in a black suit and tie, clean-shaven, and stunningly handsome. Joy's mane had been braided, and her saddle and dressage fit for royalty. Erica's heart did somersaults, but she tamped down the emotions and tried to keep moving.

She sucked in a deep breath and tried to step around Adam, resisting the urge to hug Joy. Except Adam gently grabbed one of her arms, effectively stopping her. "Erica, wait. Before you leave, you need to know all the information."

"I already know more than enough," she huffed.

Adam's warm smile confused her. "Well, then, if you know I love you, why are you leaving?"

Erica jerked back. "Come again?"

"I love you."

This wasn't the information she was talking about. "But Natalie…"

"I love Natalie as well. But God has blessed me with two perfect loves. Two completely different women, yet both beautiful, kind-hearted souls who I will love forever and ever. It's not a competition. Natalie's time was cut short, but our time, yours and mine, is just starting. Trust me, Natalie would want you and I to be happy together."

"Adam's right." Maureen Vincent stepped forward. "I'm so sorry I said all those hateful things. My Natalie loved Adam, and she would settle for nothing less than to know he was happy again."

Erica was in shock, not only because of Maureen's sincere apology, but even more so by Adam's declaration of love. Her mind was spinning with all the new and unexpected revelations.

"Will you stay…with me?" he asked.

So much for not crying. Adam's words opened the floodgates all over again. "I don't know—"

Adam smiled. "Don't know if you love me? Or if you can stay? Let me help you decide by telling you what you need to know. You can trust me. I didn't give you Joy. That was Gilly's decision, and he delivered Joy without me knowing. It came as much of a shock to me as it was to you. Well, maybe not as much. Gilly was tasked with finding Joy a new home, someone who needed hope and healing. I couldn't give Joy the time and attention she deserved, not with all the other horses that are part of my guide business. When I told Gilly about you after that first day you arrived, he took some of my comments and made the leap that you would be the perfect recipient."

Erica was stunned at the information bomb Adam had just delivered. He didn't give her Joy. The swell of emotion was overwhelming. He hadn't lied to her. "That may be so, but you knew Joy was your horse. You made a fool of me, traipsing about in the wilderness in search of...well, it turns out, in search of you," she huffed, forcing herself not to get caught up in the magic of Adam's declaration of innocence.

"Perhaps to your way of thinking, but to me, it was the only way to get you to spend time with Joy. You needed her, and I needed to help you."

"Why?"

"Because I care about you a great deal. I wasn't there for you after summer camp, and I wasn't walking away this time to leave you to fend for yourself."

"Oh." It was no more than her aunt had tried to tell her, but coming from Adam, and knowing his reasoning, well, that struck a chord of forgiveness she hadn't expected.

"Exactly. Which is why I want you to stay. And this," he gestured to the entire crowd gathered around, "this is me making a fool of myself to show you how much I love you."

Erica smiled. "I stand corrected. This now has to be the sweetest thing you've ever said to me."

"Try this on for size then." Adam dropped to one knee and held up a hand, a black velvet box open wide, and a diamond ring that glittered in the sunlight beaming up at her. "Erica Carter, will you make me the happiest man in the world and marry me?"

It was at that moment that the flurry of activity all around caught her attention. Many of the folks in the crowd held up a sign of some sort, and the signs all had one thing in common...the words...*SAY YES*.

"The town loves you and wants you to stay. I love you and want you to stay. You belong here...with me. Please tell me you've forgiven me and feel the same."

Tears ran unchecked down her face. "I don't know what to think. Everything is happening so fast, and my brain is trying to catch up, but yes, I love you, too. I think I always have. I was leaving because it seemed we didn't stand a chance together," she admitted, relief filling her as she finally said the words out loud. Words she had wanted to say for a very long time.

"There's so much to explain about what's happening with the program and Maureen, and there will be plenty of time to tell you later. What's most important now...is that I'm waiting for your answer and at the risk of being rejected, I'm asking you again...will you marry me? For today and all the tomorrows of our lives?"

"Yes. I love you so much and I still can't believe all this, but I want to marry you. I want to be your wife forever and ever."

Adam stood and slid the ring on her finger, love and joy in his eyes as he leaned down to drop a kiss on her mouth.

All around them, folks hollered and cheered with excitement.

Adam put one finger under her chin and tilted her face upward. "Believe it, darling. But the bigger question is...do you love me enough to say I do...right now?"

Erica pulled back, stunned at his question. "Now?"

"Yes. We've got the whole town as witnesses, and there's no time better than the present. I think we are well overdue. I know how I feel about you, and neither time nor anything else will change those feelings. So, it's up for you to decide. If you need more time, I can give you time. A week maybe." He grinned.

"A week? Mighty generous with your time." She laughed, shaking her head at the sudden craziness of what was happening. *Adam loved her.* Completely, irrevocably loved her. But to get married now...or even in a week...it was ludicrous no matter how much she loved the man who just asked her to marry him. "I don't even have a dress. And there are so many details that would need to be attended to. I was going on the train this morning, not on a trip to city hall. And I really don't want to get married in jeans."

Adam grinned and looked over at Aunt Mary as she stepped forward.

"That's where I come in. I know true love when I see it and it's written all over your face and the gleam in your eyes when you mention Adam's name. You two are in love, and simply needed time to talk things over. Which is why I had to run an errand this morning. The alterations on your dress took a little longer than expected, but I'm sure you'll be pleased with the results."

"My dress?" Erica asked. The surprises just kept coming.

Aunt Mary laughed. "Of course. Can't have you getting married in jeans, now, can we?"

"You knew Adam was going to propose? And that he was going to do all this?" she asked, gesturing toward the crowd.

"Yes, but I'm hoping you'll forgive me for not ruining the surprise. Just like the whole town came out today to show their support and to hope you'll forgive them for not outing Adam over Joy. He went through so much after losing Natalie and Sundancer's Joy was important to him. A very special horse indeed. And not one person here in town didn't understand the importance of Adam giving you Joy. Well, Gilly giving you Joy. But if Adam wanted secrecy regarding Joy's part in his own life, the people in town trusted him to know what was best."

It was truly a day of revelations. And forgiveness. "I forgive everyone since it was Joy who helped me emotionally reconnect with the world, not to mention, it was Joy who brought Adam and I together."

Adam wrapped his arms around Erica and lowered his head to kiss her. The entire crowd disappeared, and it was just like when they were kids. *Just the two of them*. Lost in a sea of love. The sound of clapping and cheering broke into the moment.

"So, will you marry me?"

"Yes. Yes. Yes." She wrapped her arms around his neck, still finding it hard to believe he loved her and wanted to marry her.

"Today or next week, the choice is yours? And not at city hall...in the church."

"You have that all arranged as well? Wow, you are full of surprises, but then, like I've always said, you are always prepared for everything."

"I wasn't prepared for you." He grinned.

His comment took her breath away. "In that case, my answer is today," Erica said, not wanting to miss another minute of life with the man of her dreams. And her heart.

"I was hoping you would come around and see it my way." Adam scooped her up in his arms and deposited her in the saddle on Joy. He took the lead rope and led the horse to the church, the town's people all following. It was a wedding procession fit for a queen.

Erica couldn't stop the tears, and when they arrived at the church, Adam helped her down and escorted her up the steps, where the pastor waited.

"You were awfully sure of yourself, Mr. Landon," she teased.

Adam shook his head. "Not at all. In fact, I was a nervous wreck. I was putting all my faith in God, and in you, and what I suspected was your love for me."

"As long as you always have that faith, I reckon we will be golden."

"Sounds perfect. From now until our golden years." Adam grinned.

Hand in hand, they entered the church. "Not so fast aging us. Let's enjoy the journey."

"Absolutely, my beautiful bride. Now hurry and change so we can get married, and then go home to start our journey together."

"Yes, dear."

"I like the sound of that," Adam teased.

"So do I, Mr. Landon. So do I."

Chapter Twenty

♥

Erica couldn't believe this was happening. One minute she was leaving town, the next she was staying. And getting married.

To Adam.

Her aunt came into the room, a white dress in her arms. She held it up for Erica's inspection. "What do you think, dear?"

The scalloped neckline, white lace with delicate flowers woven into the pattern, covered the satiny gown. The tapered midsection accentuated the waist, and flowing folds that hung to the ground were t-length in the front and floor length in the back. "It's gorgeous," she said, letting her hand caress the fine material. "I can't believe this is my wedding dress." It was perfect and exactly what she would have chosen for herself.

"Believe it. It's my way of making everything up to you," Aunt Mary said, her beaming smile a sight to behold.

Erica should have known her aunt's strange attitude this morning was all a ruse. But lost in her own shroud of darkness, she hadn't thought it through with much clarity. "Oh, Aunt Mary, you've outdone yourself, and then some. You are so forgiven for everything." Erica twirled in front of the mirror, holding up the dress. It was like a fairy princess moment and not one she wanted to forget.

"I'll help you slip it on. And there are shoes to match," she said, pointing to a box on the bench.

Erica was thrilled and stepped out of her jeans and pulled her T-shirt over her head. "It's a good thing my bra will work." She laughed. Her aunt helped slip the skirt and bodice over her head, pulled the skirt down, and adjusted the folds of silken material. After zipping up the back, she moved away, examining the total effect of the dress.

"Simply lovely. Look, dear."

Erica couldn't believe the vision staring back at her. It was one thing to hold the dress up, quite another to see it on. The woman in the mirror radiated with love. It was perfect. "I love it." She hugged her aunt, careful not to step on the hem of the dress and trip.

"Wonderful. Put on your shoes, and there's a small tiara in the box as well. Your hair is perfect. Oh, and I've got a necklace for you. The aquamarine necklace will look lovely, and it can be considered something borrowed and something blue." Her aunt retrieved the pendant from her purse.

"Aunt Mary, you've thought of everything to make this special. I don't know how to thank you."

"I'm glad you think so. And you can thank us by being happy. Live life to the fullest with Adam by your side. We best get going though, as I'm not so sure your husband-to-be won't come searching for you if you don't make an appearance soon. Can't have him see the gown before you're ready. Your uncle will be right outside the door to escort you down the aisle."

"I just can't believe this. It's like a fairytale." Erica dabbed at the tears rolling down her cheeks with a tissue.

"So, you're not upset at the haste? I worried you would want to plan a wedding," her aunt asked, suddenly serious.

"Not at all. This is far more interesting and memorable. Knowing everything Adam put together in case I said yes tells me far more than words how much he loves me."

Her aunt nodded. "That he does. Let's get a move on. We've got a wedding to attend."

Erica took her uncle's arm, and they stood at the entrance to the sanctuary. Her aunt moved to the front pew and signaled for the music to begin. Folks from town had filled the small church to overflowing capacity.

She was truly home and a part of the community.

The music started. Erica walked toward Adam, love filling her heart with joy and peace. This was all very real. She smiled, tears threatening to spill over yet again. She wiped them away, not wanting to miss a single moment of the happiest day of her life.

Her uncle kissed her cheek and then took her hand and placed it in Adam's.

"Hey, beautiful. You are the loveliest bride I've ever seen and I'm so glad you didn't change your mind." Adam shot her a wink, his warm smile all she needed as a reflection of his feelings.

"Never. I love you," Erica said, unable to stop the tears.

Adam pulled a tissue from his jacket pocket and dabbed at the tears. "I love you, too."

They turned to face the pastor, more than ready to declare their vows of commitment to one another. The minutes flew by and they were pronounced husband and wife.

Forever and ever.

Adam still couldn't believe Erica had said yes. More than that, his beautiful bride was smiling and laughing, and the light in her eyes was the same one he remembered when they were kids. "May I have this dance?"

"For the rest of our lives," Erica said, taking his arm.

Adam kissed his wife before leading her to the dance floor, not caring that everyone was watching. *His wife.* He loved the sound of the words, but he loved Erica even more. "Our first dance."

"Second."

"What—" he asked.

"We danced under a moonlit sky at camp after we snuck out of our cabins one night. Don't tell me you forgot."

"How could I forget? It's the night I kissed you."

"A memorable night, for sure. Just like this moment. Our forever memory. You do, however, realize I can't dance. There wasn't much call for dancing in the military."

"Trust me to lead, and you'll be fine."

"I'm all yours." Adam smiled down at his bride and swept her close, before spinning her away in a graceful waltz. The happiness reflected in Erica's eyes would fill his soul for a long time. He understood, more than ever, how precious every day was, and he vowed to make the most of his life with Erica.

By the time the waltz finished, throngs of other couples had joined them on the dance floor.

"You can dance. Nice to know." Erica grinned.

"It's easy with you. Why don't we head over to the cake? I'm kind of hungry."

"I still can't believe you did all this, and in such a short time."

"The whole town pitched in once I pleaded my case. Word spreads quickly in a small town."

"So, it would seem."

They moved to the cake and Mary appeared by their side. "Give me a minute. I'll make an announcement to get everyone gathered around before you cut the cake."

"What flavor?"

"What flavor, what?" Adam asked, knowing what she meant, but savoring the moment.

"The cake, of course." Erica grinned. "I'm kind of partial to chocolate."

"A little birdy told me something different was called for today."

"Do tell," she said, leaning closer to hear.

"Peanut butter and jelly."

Erica threw her head back and laughed. "No way. But perfect. Can't wait to try it."

"Oh, you will. Trust me." Who knew planning a whirlwind wedding could be such fun?

"We're going to play fair, right? None of the *in-your-face shenanigans*."

"I like fair." Which, to Adam's way of thinking, included all the rights and traditions of a normal wedding reception.

True to her word, Mary got the guests all gathered around. "Silence everyone. The happy couple would like to say a few words."

Adam cleared his throat. "I just want to thank everyone for your help in putting this together, all without even knowing Erica would marry me. Your faith in me, and in the love Erica and I share, is such a blessing. So, without further ado, it's time to cut the cake."

The crowd cheered them on as they took hold of the cake cutter, his hand wrapped over hers as they sliced a piece. *Together.*

Erica pulled off a small section of the cake and held it out to him. He leaned down and ate the cake from her fingers, grasping her hand and kissing the same fingers seconds later. Adam took a slightly bigger section and held it out to Erica.

She leaned forward to take a bite, but Adam darted his hand upward and swiped at her nose.

Erica jumped back. "You promised," she said, wiping her nose and laughing.

"I promised to be fair. Fair enough to give our guests the fun and games they came for." Adam shot her a wink. He turned to wave at the crowd, high fiving the air.

He turned back just as Erica smashed the rest of the slice of cake in his face, twisting her hand to make sure he was good and covered. *Little minx.* Adam grabbed her by the hand and kissed her. No light kiss, the kind that made sure they shared everything...including the white frosting, and red jelly, and peanut butter cake.

Amidst laughter and cheers, Aunt Mary tapped them on the shoulder. She handed them both a napkin, her own smile from ear to ear. "Nice work, you two. Messy, but nice."

"Sounds like a recipe for life. Messy but nice. I like it," Erica said.

"Anything with you sounds perfect, darling."

Married life in the first month was hectic, as Erica spent most of the time getting settled in her new home. It had been a whirlwind of activity and there was no time for a honeymoon. *Not yet anyway.* Adam had promised her a beachy honeymoon somewhere romantic after the Sidekick Squad Connection's grand opening when Tamila would take over as the new director.

Except, in another unique twist of events, Tamila instead opted to continue the assistant's position after Maureen Vincent signed on to work with the program, preferring Maureen take on the lead role as director. Under Maureen's leadership, Erica knew the program would be in excellent hands for years and years to come. And when Adam had asked Erica about sponsoring a child, she had been completely on board. The foundation was a worthy cause, and it meant so much to Adam, but also to her.

Natalie's vision had been very grandiose in design, and the calling wasn't one Erica could ignore. At first, she was hesitant to mention it to Adam, worried he might think she was overstepping her bounds. But as always, his love and support were never ending, and he was wholeheartedly on board with her taking a more active role in the program. She was detail oriented and driven for success, which made her the perfect person to handle the full-time fund-raising aspect.

Today was the day they had all been waiting for...Adam more so than everyone else. Other than Natalie herself. Erica truly believed Natalie could see her dream coming true and would love what Adam had done to make her dream become a reality.

Adam drove to the community center where today's meeting would take place. He parked the truck, and they joined the large group of adults and children hovering around outside the gym. They spotted Maureen and went to stand by her.

"Good morning, Maureen. Are you excited about today?" Adam asked.

"I am. I've been matched with a thir-teen-year-old girl by the name of Rose. I'm taking her to the flower gardens over in Willow and then we will have a nice luncheon. It will give us a chance to relax and get to know one another."

"That sounds lovely. Adam and I are picking up an eight-year-old boy by the name of Trevor. His mother is going through a difficult divorce and after much discussion, we've agreed to keep him for a week at the ranch. Irene was thrilled with the offer and given that Adam was the founder of the program, felt as though he was clearly trustwor-thy," Erica said.

"What a wonderful thing to do for the child. I can't wait to hear how it goes. Maybe that's something I could do at some point. You know, like keeping a child for a week. There's so much space at my place...and I've got Natalie's old room. I never changed it, and I see no reason to now." There was a hint of wistfulness to the older woman's voice, but Erica understood the emo-tions that would come from losing someone you loved. She was glad they were all friends now, as it made life easier.

"I think that's a great idea. And perhaps we should look into the logistics of making it a regular option as part of the program. It would be like a summer camp instead of a weekend getaway."

"Let's get through this week and see if we all feel the same way," Adam teased.

"Good idea. I see Tamila waving at us. Looks like it's time to match up our kids and adults. What an exciting time," Erica said.

"Thank you for being you. And agreeing to be my wife." Adam kissed her cheek.

"You're quite welcome. Good thing you asked me. I don't even like to think what I'd be doing today if you hadn't."

"You'd be bored and lonely without me," he teased, shooting her one of his charming winks.

"Probably." Erica headed toward the front of the group to stand with Tamila and Maureen.

Maureen stepped up to the microphone. "Thank you all for coming as we kick off the first Sidekick Squad Connections. I can never thank Adam enough for his perseverance in setting everything up, against all odds...including yours truly. As you know, I'm the new program director. I look forward to hearing from all of you as we continue to grow and develop." The older woman shot him a grin as the grownups chuckled. "I can feel the excitement in the air. So many adults signed up, and it's a good thing with all the kids enrolled in the program. Everyone's on board with the current list of approved activities and I can't wait to hear more ideas, so be sure to start brainstorming. It's been suggested we add a week-long camp option, so the more ideas we have, the better. And be sure to let us know if you would be interested in the possibility. Without further ado, Adam, will you do the honor of announcing the first connections and making the introductions?"

Adam stepped up to the mic, waving at the crowd. "Thanks, Maureen. In the end, God's plan for the program prevailed. With Him on our side, we couldn't lose. So here we go. As I call out your names, if the kid and the adult will step forward and introduce themselves, then you can move off to the side and meet with the parent or guardian in attendance." The matching program was quite extensive, so Erica doubted they would run into problems.

Her husband was in his element as he called out the names, leaving Trevor for last. They had already met the boy in order to make the arrangements for the extra time they would spend together. Hiking and fishing were on the menu, but then so was horseback riding...an activity his mother signed off on. What the kid didn't know was that he would ride Joy. The extra time would give them all the opportunity to form a stronger bond.

Adam moved to stand with Trevor and his mother, while Erica and Tamila took over answering questions so that Maureen could talk with Lily, her connection child. After everyone left and questions were answered, she met back up with Trevor and Adam. "Ready to head to the ranch?" she asked.

"I've been ready. Are you really going to teach me to fish and ride?" Trevor asked, his voice filled with excitement.

"We are. And tonight, as part of the welcome to our home, we've planned an outdoor barbeque, complete with a campfire for roasting marshmallows." Erica placed one hand on Trevor's shoulder as they turned to head for the parking lot.

"*Ummm*, I don't know how to roast a marsh-mallow," Trevor mumbled, the words barely audible, as though he were embarrassed to admit such a thing.

"That's okay. You will after tonight. Everyone has to learn things they've never done when the time is right. This week you will learn lots of new things, and it's okay if you don't get it right or aren't good at something. It's part of the learning curve," Adam said. He was taking the man-to-man conversation in stride.

More like father-son.

"What Trevor doesn't know yet is that I like to burn my marshmallows...on purpose." Erica grinned.

"Burned?" Trevor asked, scrunching up his face in dislike.

"Say it isn't so," Adam chimed in, shaking his head in disbelief.

Erica nodded. "To a crisp."

"Don't worry, Trevor. I'll show you how to roast a perfect golden marshmallow and how to make a smore. It requires patience...something I feel Erica doesn't have much of."

"Me? You're the one who asked me to marry him and whisked me off down the aisle ten minutes later."

"No way," Trevor said, looking back and forth between them.

"Yes, way," Erica confirmed.

"You complaining?" Adam asked, stepping closer, a grin on his face.

"Not a chance. But I'm just pointing out...your rush to get married isn't any different from my rush to blacken a marshmallow. It's a sign of impatience."

"Point taken, Mrs. Landon."

Adam leaned in to kiss her before she slid into the car.

"Gross. I didn't know you two just got married. Does that mean I'm going to have to put up with lots of yucky kissing and handholding?" Trevor asked.

"Get used to it, kid. I love my wife."

Trevor rolled his eyes and then slid into the middle seat of the truck.

As for Erica, she looked forward to what the future would hold, because they were off to a great start and agreed on all the important things. *Like loving each other.*

Sundancer's Joy had originally been Adam's blessing, but then he'd given the mare to Erica. And Joy continued to help all the children that came to the ranch. Patient and understanding, Joy was a beautiful mare with a beautiful spirit to give love and healing to everyone she met.

To Joy's accolades, they added the ability to bring two hurting souls together and help them discover the ultimate happiness in love. And most importantly, *Sundancer's Legacy was a pay-it-forward legacy.* A tradition they were in the process of fulfilling. This spring Joy was scheduled to be bred, and when her first foal was ready, they would start the search for the right person who needed hope and healing. Someone who would love the horse and honor the legacy. Someone who needed *Sundancer's Heart,* the name he and Erica had decided on for Joy's first foal and the next in line as part of the legacy.

And about that time, they'd have their hands full with a baby of their own. They had been shocked to learn Erica was pregnant not long after they were married but couldn't have been happier.

Noah after Adam's father. Or Natalie. It was still too soon to tell.

The girl's name had been Erica's suggestion, and Adam agreed. His love continued to deepen every day at the depth of her understanding and gentle spirit. No man deserved to have this much love in his life, but he was grateful to God for giving him a second chance at happiness.

***

If you enjoyed this sweet and charming romance, be sure to check out the ALSO BY ELSIE DAVIS section on the next page for more clean and wholesome romance. Next up – Book 3 – Sundancer's Heart

Want to keep in touch with new releases and what's happening in the world of Elsie Davis?

Sign up for the monthly newsletter at Elsie Davi s.com

The greatest compliment you could give an author is to leave a review in order to help other readers discover the same great stories you enjoyed. Amazon/Bookbub/Goodreads are all great places. Many thanks!!!

Another great way to keep in touch - ***Follow Elsie Davis on FaceBook***

About The Author

Elsie Davis is a *USA Today and International Bestselling Author* of over 30 sweet, clean, and wholesome romances, and a member of the ACFW. She discovered the world of Happily-Ever-After romance at the age of twelve when she began avidly reading Barbara Cartland, the Queen of Romance, and has been hooked ever since. After building her dream log home on top of a small mountain, she turned her attention to do what she loves most, writing. Elsie writes sweet Contemporary Romance and Contemporary Christian Romance from her heart...hoping to share a little love in a big world.

When she's not writing, she can be found birding, kayaking, camping, fishing, playing disc golf, and taking nature walks—hoping to spot wildlife. Basically, she loves all things outdoors, EXCEPT cold weather. She and her husband are avid Caribbean cruisers, but Elsie's favorite vacation was their cruise to Alaska. (In spite of the cold!) Indoors, she enjoys a toasty fire, and of course, a great romance with a guaranteed Happily-Ever-After.

https://www.elsiedavis.com

Also By Elsie Davis

Sweet, Clean, and Wholesome Stories...with a Happily-Ever-After Guarantee!

Great Smoky Mountain Getaways
(Christian Inspirational – Women's Fiction Romances)
Juliet's Journey to Love
Poppy's Path to Love
Rachel's Road to Love
Taylor's Trek to Love
Grace's Getaway to Love – 2025
Dixie's Detour to Love – 2025
Angel's Adventure to Love – 2025

Crossroads Creek Cowboys
(Christian Inspirational Romances)
The Heart of a Cowboy
The Help of a Cowboy
The Return of a Cowboy
The Care of a Cowboy
The Dream of a Cowboy – 2024
The Life of a Cowboy – 2024
The Tears of a Cowboy – 2025

Holidays in Hallbrook
(Sweet Romance Series for Holidays Throughout
the Year)
***Welcome to Hallbrook, New Hampshire. A
small-town filled with the unexpected, lots of
love, and of course, a beloved dog to ramp up
the excitement.***
Love & Order (Labor Day)
Love & Family (Thanksgiving)
Love & Peace (Christmas)
Love & Chocolate (Valentine's Day)
Love & Hope (Mother's Day)
Love & Liberty (Independence Day)

Love & Honor (Veteran's Day)
Love & Joy (Easter)
Love & Adventure (Father's Day)
Lov & Cheer (New Year's Day – TBD)

Sundancer's Legacy

(Contemporary Christian Romance)

Sundancer's Star

Sundancer's Joy
Sundancer's Heart – 2025

2025/2026
Sundancer's Majesty
Sundancer's Miracle
Sundancer's Glory
Sundancer's Kiss
Sundancer's Moon
Sundancer's Splendor

Trinity River Romances
(Sweet Western Romance)
Ranchers and farmers depend on the Trinity River for water, but when a secret conglomerate starts buying up property by fair means or foul, it's time for the landowners of Tumble County to fight back—Texas style. But what they don't count on, is finding love in the process.
Back in the Rancher's Arms
Small Town, Big Secrets
The Firefighter's Miscalculation (2025)
Love Advice for the Cowboy (2026)

Crestfield Inn Romances
If you like special kinds of soulmates, a splash of the supernatural, and wholesome relationships, you'll adore this sweet bit of fun filled with romance and mystery.
Turning Back Time
Turning Up Roses
Turning Down Pie

Celebrity Corgi Romance
(Standalone Sweet Romance/Light Mystery)
If you like light mystery mixed in with your happily-ever-after, you'll enjoy this second-chance romance and the race to save an adorable Corgi.
Digging the Driver

Gold Coast Retrievers
(Standalone Sweet Romance/Light Mystery)
Special Golden Retrievers help their humans solve mysteries, save lives, and even find love...
Defending Dakota

9 781959 401094